AGENTS OF THE ABYSS

DETECTIVES OF THE ABYSS

John L. French Patrick Thomas

PADWOLF
PUBLISHING

PADWOLF PUBLISHING INC.
WWW.PADWOLF.COM
www.facebook.com/Padwolf

www.theagentsoftheabyss.com

DETECTIVES OF THE ABYSS
by
John L. French and Patrick Thomas
© 2023 Patrick Thomas

cover by Patrick Thomas

*Agents of the Abyss created by Patrick Thomas and all related characters
and settings are © and ™ Patrick Thomas*

ISBN 978-1-958310-02-1
FIrst Printing.

To Kevin Meares,
Good friend and ghost hunter extraordinaire

1

Where There's a Will

It was late autumn 1938. The Second Martian War was over but the activities of Germany's National Socialist Party had me wondering if another great war was about to begin.

"The signs are all there, my dear Jane," Sherlock Holmes said from his chair as if reading my mind. He has done this so often that I have ceased to be surprised or to even comment on it. "There's another east wind blowing for those who have the wit to see. The question is which countries will become involved and which side they will be on."

"Let us hope that Transylvania stays out of it, Uncle."

"It will be devasting if he does not. But I believe the Count will maintain his neutrality."

"He calls himself a king these days."

"He will always be a count to me, Jane, if only because that title annoys him so. But back to the matter at hand."

I was with my godfather Sherlock Holmes in his Baker Street apartment discussing the possibility that the French criminal Fantômas had moved his operations to England. Holmes was sitting in his usual chair while I occupied the one so often used by my late father, Doctor John Watson.

My godfather was in his eighties and, while still active, did more consulting than adventuring. He left that to his "Irregulars" and sometimes to me when I could be spared from my medical duties at the London School of Medicine for Women.

"Scotland Yard believes that Fantômas may be in league with Erik of Paris."

Holmes shook his head. "Of course, they do. They are fooled by the similarities of the names. However, I don't see those two working together. True, while their methods of operation may be similar in nature, Fantômas's talent for disguise is natural. The Opera Ghost's however …" He gave a shudder. "There are those who say what I do …" I gave him a look. "Very well, what *we* do is magic. What Erik does, however …" He shook his head. "They call it science, but it is somehow akin to supernatural. No matter. Sooner or later the science of detection will catch up with our friend Fantômas. There are some things he cannot disguise. Which reminds me, tomorrow night I am lecturing at Scotland Yard on bloodstain patterns. Would you like to come? I can promise quite a mess."

Before I could answer there was a knock on the door. "Yes, Miss Hudson, what is it?" he called out.

"Sorry to bother you, Mr. Holmes, but there's a lady to see you."

Holmes and I looked at each other. "Are you expecting someone, Uncle?"

"Not at my age, Jane."

"Maybe it's a client? Possibly my neighbor on Praed Street is busy."

He ignored me. "Send her in, Miss Hudson."

Soon the door was opened and our landlady's niece announced Emily Harrison.

"Do come in, Miss Harrison, and be seated. Do forgive my not getting up. It is poor circulation and not ill-manners that keep me from rising. May I introduce my associate, Dr. Jane Morstan Watson."

Miss Harrison looked confused. How had Sherlock Holmes known she was unmarried and why was Doctor Watson a woman? As to the first question, like Holmes, I too had noticed the lack of a wedding band and there was no telltale sign that one had been recently removed. As for the second question,

"Doctor Watson here is the daughter of my old friend and companion who has passed on. I assure you that she is every bit as capable as her father in assisting me with whatever problem you might have. Speaking of which …"

At Holmes's prompt, Miss Harrison said, "It's not the kind of problem that would appear in the Strand. It is instead a personal problem. As I was in the city already, I thought to seek your advice on the matter."

Leaning back in his chair, Holmes tented his fingers and said, "Please, proceed."

"I am engaged to one Percy Covington. My father, Roger Harrison, does not approve of this engagement. In fact, he is very much against it to the point of threatening to have Percy arrested if he comes to Harrison Hall."

"Which is why you're in the city, Miss Harrison," I asked, "to meet Mr. Covington."

"Yes."

"Does he know about your coming here?"

"We have no secrets from each other."

That prompted a chuckle from my godfather. "Come now, Miss Harrison. We all have and keep secrets, even from ourselves. But I do believe that you told your fiancé about your coming here, that he thinks nothing will come from your visit, but supports your effort anyway, as any man in love should."

"How did you know, Mr. Holmes?"

Uncle merely shook his head. Except to make a point, he gave up explaining his deductions years ago. I had my ideas on how he knew but they would wait until after our client left.

"Why is your father against Mr. Covington?"

"Percy is an artist, Mr. Holmes. You've probably never heard his name for he does not exhibit in the galleries, but he makes his living in portraiture, both traditional and photographic."

"And your father objects because your fiancé is in the arts."

"Yes, that and because my brother Lionel has used his poison tongue to turn my father against him."

"Let me guess your problem, Miss Harrison. Thanks to your brother, your father has or plans to change his will to disinherit you if you marry Percy Covington. As you are a woman in love, you plan on marrying him anyway. That will leave your bother sole heir. Am I correct?

Miss Harrison nodded. "Yes, Mr. Holmes. In fact, my father has already changed it."

"Is money an issue? Should you marry, will you and your

husband suffer due to its lack?"

"No, Percy earns enough to support us, but …"

Holmes smiled. "These days one can never have enough money. And there's a principle involved besides. Your brother should not be allowed to profit by his bad behavior."

"Exactly, Mr. Holmes. Can you help me?"

"Possibly. Have you seen a copy of your father's will?"

"Yes."

"And does it specifically state that you will receive no inheritance should you marry Percy Covington."

"Yes."

"And does it also state that by accepting your inheritance you agree never to marry Percy Covington, on penalty of forfeiture of the entire amount?"

"Yes."

Holmes clapped his hands. "Excellent. Then Doctor Watson and I can definitely help you. There's just one thing?"

He named a figure. I thought it a bit high and from the look on Miss Harrison's face so did she. Possibly she believed that Sherlock Holmes worked *pro bono*, but as she herself admitted, one can never have too much money.

"Ten percent will do as a retainer, Miss Harrison, the rest payable on results."

A reluctant but desperate Miss Harrison wrote a cheque for the required amount and departed, leaving Holmes and me alone. As soon as she left he went to the window. I joined him in time to watch her embrace what could only be her fiancé.

"You saw him from the window."

"Of course, Jane. Despite how some of those unauthorized stories depict me, I am not clairvoyant. Now then I suppose you have already figured out the solution to our client's problem."

"It was elementary. In fact, there are two possible solutions."

"You did notice the crucifix around Miss Harrison's neck."

"Ah, yes. So that leaves only one solution. But they'll have to be discrete."

"I believe they can be, Jane. But that's not what worries me.

Where there is enough money to scheme over, there is enough to kill over. If I were young Harrison, I would worry about my father changing his mind."

"And take preemptive action?" Holmes nodded. "But surely he can't expect to get away with it. Not in these days of modern policing."

"And not with Sherlock Holmes on the case."

I had to correct him. "Sherlock Holmes and Doctor Watson."

"In any case, Jane, look up the elder Harrison's solicitor and find out who, if anyone, is heir after Lionel. And let us hope that, for once, I am wrong."

The following day, my godfather being busy at Scotland Yard, it fell to me to set up a meeting with Miss Harrison and Mr. Covington to give them our solution to their problem.

"That's remarkably simple," Covington said in surprise.

"Simple yet expensive," I said. "In addition to Mr. Holmes's fee, there will be other expenditures. But with our connections, it should be done by next week. I must caution the two of you, however, to be discrete. You would not want word to leak out."

"We understand. Not a word until, well, never mind. Separate lives then, Percy," Miss Harrison said to her fiancé.

"At least on the surface, my dear."

"The 'until' Miss Harrison nearly spoke of occurred sooner than anyone other than Sherlock Holmes had expected. Three weeks later, after I had finished my rounds at the School of Medicine I received a telephone call. It was my godfather.

"Jane, the game is afoot," he said in an excited voice, which told me that there was a crime to be investigated, most probably murder.

"Harrison Hall, I assume?"

"Where else? It's the only case we have at present, until Fantômas shows his head."

"Or someone else's. How did you hear of it?"

"Wiggins called me from the Yard. He has the case. He'll meet you at the Hall."

Wiggins was one of Uncle's original Irregulars. He's now a Scotland Yard Inspector. One who thinks he knows more of my godfather's methods than he really does.

"Will you be there, Uncle?"

"For this, I think not. I've trained you well. Just remember one thing."

"Which is?"

"Trust no one."

"Of course not. How many steps to 221B?"

"Eighteen."

That was incorrect. It was supposed to be. We start at twelve, go up to twenty then down again, making sure to avoid the correct answer. And no, I'm not telling you what that is. My father already has.

I arrived at Harrison Hall to be greeted by a smiling Wiggins who said, "Sorry to call you out, Dr. Watson, but the case is already solved. The senior Harrison appears to have been stabbed in his sleep. We're about to arrest his son."

"You found a knife in Lionel's room?" I asked as Wiggins stepped aside to admit me. "And Miss Harrison no doubt told you about the will?"

Wiggins looked flustered. "Well, yes as to the knife. How did you know the son's name or about the will?"

"You know his methods, Wiggins. You should apply them as I do. Now then, was it his sister who told you?"

"No, it was his cousin Adrian, who is visiting along with his wife Agatha."

Oh, Wiggins, how disappointed my godfather would be with you. "Anyone else in the house who could have killed Harrison and hidden the knife in Lionel's room?"

With that question, Wiggins realized the chasm of conclusion he had leapt in ascribing ownership of the knife. He nodded and said, "Geoffrey Fisher, the family solicitor was here when the body was discovered. And Miss Harrison's fiancé, Percy Covington, has just arrived."

Too many suspects. I began to think that I would be gathering the lot of them into the living room to reveal the killer. The lights would go out, there would be a panic-inducing gunshot, then the killer would run into the burly constable I'll have placed just outside the door for just such an occurrence.

"Show me the body," I said and Wiggins led me upstairs to Harrison's room.

Before entering I examined the door. No signs of force. "Please tell me the door wasn't locked before the body was found."

Wiggins shook his head. "According to the servants, Harrison never locked his door. He said that since his wife died, he had no reason to."

Anyone coming into the room would have thought Harrison asleep. A closer examination would have revealed the penetrating stab wound over the heart. "And the knife?" I asked.

"*In situ* where we found it when we searched the house. In Lionel Harrison's bedroom, in a desk drawer. Silly place to hide a murder weapon."

"Only if it's your bedroom. Now them, Wiggins, please excuse me while I examine the body."

Wiggins stepped out, leaving a constable at the door. Putting on thin rubber gloves, I went to work and soon confirmed the suspected cause of death. I then put aside my medical training and fell back on the teachings of my godfather. I made a hands and knees examination of the bedroom floor, unfortunately not finding the collar button or stray scrap of lace that would identify the killer. Then from my bag, I removed my tools of scientific detection and again went to work.

When I was finished Harrison's bedroom was dirtier than it had been and the constable at the door pointed out a grey smudge of powder on my cheek. I thanked him, wiped it off, and went to examine the knife.

It was the right size and shape to have caused the wound. I swabbed what little blood there was on the blade for eventual ABO typing and comparison with Harrison's blood type. I then dirtied the knife, the desk, and for good measure the room door, in the process again smudging my cheek.

I met Wiggins downstairs and asked, "Where are the suspects?"

"The servants are confined to their quarters under guard.

Family and friends are in the drawing-room, under guard and with instructions not to discuss the case."

"Very good, Wiggins. Now let's find our murderer."

We entered. Wiggins introduced me but it was not until I mentioned that I was acting in the name of Sherlock Holmes that I was afforded any kind of respect or authority.

"Mr. Fisher," I began, "you came here this morning at Mr. Harrison's request in reference to his will, did you not?"

"Eh, yes, Miss Watson, but how did you …"

"That doesn't matter, and it is Doctor Watson, if you please. Was it to revoke the one he previously made or to correct an oversight?"

"The latter I'm afraid. But of course …"

"Owing to his death, the correction wasn't made."

"No, it wasn't."

I glanced over to Miss Harrison who gave me a nod and a slight smile. All was good, she no doubt thought, not realizing that she and her fiancé were now higher on the suspect list.

"And to the best of your knowledge, did Mister Harrison discuss this correction with anyone other than you?"

"He said he had not."

"Very good." I did my best to convey an "air of omniscience" as I looked around the room.

"Always let them believe you know more than you do, Jane," Holmes frequently told me when he was instructing me in the art of detection. "They will often tell you things they think you already know."

"Mister Harrison, Miss Harrison, did any of you know what this correction might be?"

"No," Miss Harrison answered, "Father merely said that Mr. Fisher would be here this morning. I assumed it was about a business matter."

"Which would have been handled in his business office. No, Miss Harrison, Mr. Harrison, this was a personal matter and either or both of you may have guessed what it was and taken lethal action."

Before they could protest my implication, I turned to Adrian and Agatha. "Who invited you?"

"It was Lionel," Agatha answered. She was a tall woman who towered over her husband. That she answered for him gave me a hint at the dynamics of their marriage. "He said that it had been too long since we visited and invited us to stay through the weekend."

"And did he happen to mention the terms of his father's most recent will?"

Adrian blushed and looked toward Miss Harrison and her fiancé. "He did mention it," he said quietly, "but of course, I had no hopes or expectations."

"But if Miss Harrison were to marry Percy Covington, and if her brother Lionel was found ineligible to inherit, well, a thrust in the dark, a planted knife, and the two of you are that much richer."

An enraged Agatha rose from her seat. "How dare you suggest …"

"I dare because I am Doctor Jane Morstan Watson, goddaughter to Sherlock Holmes, and I have the killer in the palm of my hand."

That silenced her and cowed the rest. I waited to see if the killer would break and run into the arms of the burly constable, but no, the murderer had decided to brazen it out.

I did have the killer in the palm of my hand, between the fingers of my left hand, actually. The murderer's identity was on several white cards containing fingerprints in grey powder. Prints from Lionel's bedroom door and desk. Prints from Roger Harrison's bedroom door. And prints from his headboard, which was touched when the killer leaned over to stab Harrison. And a print from the knife blade, which matched one of the prints from the headboard. Yes, I had the identity of the murderer in my grasp.

But even without a comparison, I had a sense of who it was.

"Leaving a bloody knife in someone's bedroom is a good way of implicating him in a crime. Clumsily hiding such a knife in your own room is a good way of implicating everyone but you."

I turned and looked at my suspect. "And inviting the heirs presumptive to visit then handing them a motive to kill your father and frame you is just plain foolish. Lionel Harrison, may I please see your hands? I'd like to compare your fingerprints to those of the killer's."

Lionel was more than willing to present his hands. He rushed at me in an attempt to wrap them around my throat. But my uncle had taught me more than detection and deduction. Before the burly constable could react, I threw Lionel to the ground with a *bartitsu* move.

As he was being led out, Lionel Harrison had a parting shot. "You lose as well, sister, either the man you love or father's money."

"Hold up, Constable, Inspector," Miss Morrison cried. "I have an announcement to make. Two weeks ago Percy and I were married."

Lionel's "Ha" was drowned out by Agatha's "Adrian, we get all the money." Their enjoyment was short-lived when Percy explained. "Before we got married, at the advice and with the assistance of Doctor Watson, I legally changed my last name to Bradbury. It was my mother's maiden name."

"So you see," Miss Harrison, now Mrs. Bradbury continued, "I did not marry Percy Covington but rather Percy Bradbury."

The suddenly bereft Agatha turned to Mr. Fisher. "Can they do that?"

Fisher nodded. "According to the language in the will they can. That was the correction Roger wished to make."

The formalities over, all reports made and the evidence turned over to Wiggins, who would no doubt follow in Lestrade's footsteps and claim the credit for himself, I made my way back to Baker Street where my godfather was torturing his violin in an attempt to force it to play "The Maple Leaf Rag."

"Well done, Jane," he said after I made my report. "And Lionel Harrison will go the gallows knowing that not only did his precipitative action tie the nose around his neck but also caused his sister to inherit. But I trust you did not forget the most important matter of the whole case."

"Of course not, Uncle," I said, handing him the cheque Mr. Bradbury, formerly Covington, had written me. "And don't you forget, half of that is mine."

2

Interlude
1940–The Taking of Fantômas

The man in the flat had thought himself safe, his crimes undetected or at least ascribed to another. Then came the knock on the door and the cry of, "Police, open the door, please." Still, the man believed that he had the advantage. The British police did not arm themselves. He, on the other hand …

Picking up a pistol from a table, he prepared himself to shoot the first constable through the door. That would give him time to flee through the window.

But no, noises on the fire escape told him that that means of escape was blocked. No matter, there was always a way out.

The door gave under the shoulder of a burly sergeant. The man raised his pistol and prepared to fire at the unarmed police. But the first person through the door was a slender, dark-haired woman who entered quickly, moved to one side, and trained her own firearm at him.

"Lest you wish to meet your maker sooner than you have planned, I would not do that, Monsieur Fantômas."

Fantômas, master criminal of all of Europe. He had fooled the police of several countries and bedeviled the *gendarmes* of Paris. And here he was in a London apartment, held at bay by a young woman holding a revolver that seemed much too big for her. But she was holding it steady, with the barrel in line with his heart.

Slowly, very slowly, he placed his pistol on the table. Then, hands raised, he moved to the center of the room. Giving a slight bow, he said,

"May I have the honour of knowing your name, *Mademoiselle*?"

"I am Doctor Jane Watson, goddaughter of Sherlock Holmes."

Fantômas smiled. "Of course, only the great detective or

someone he had trained could have captured one such as I. But unfortunately, *Ma Cherie*, I must bid you *adieu*."

An object dropped from Fantômas's hand. When it hit the floor, smoke burst from it. At the same time, Fantômas stamped hard upon a certain section of the floor. When the smoke disappeared …

He was still standing in the apartment with his arms raised with pistols, revolvers, and at least one shotgun pointed at him.

"Didn't you hear the doctor?" asked a tall man dressed in plain clothes, "She's the goddaughter of Sherlock Holmes. Didn't you think she'd know enough to inspect the rooms below and nail shut your trap door?"

"Inspector Wiggins?"

"Yes, Jane, rather, Doctor Watson?"

"Make sure you bind him tightly, hands and feet. Use the cuffs Holmes gave you, the ones without keys, the ones that have to be cut off. Houdini himself could not escape those. I know, I watched him try. Should he try, shoot him. I would suggest that you shoot him anyway, but his fate is for a court to decide and the hangman to carry out."

Fantômas considered himself a man without fear. But the disappointment he had seen on Doctor Watson's face when he put down his pistol and the look she was now giving him as she coolly discussed his extra-legal execution frightened him. Perhaps, this time there were no means of escape.

"I assure you, Inspector, I will remain in your custody." *I can always escape from prison,* he thought. *It would not be the first time.*

3

The Ghost of Thornfax Manor

War. In that fateful year of 1938, death had once again come from above. This time the invaders had learned from their defeat two decades prior and had prepared against the pathogens that had defeated them the first time.

But humanity, and some that had no claim to be included among their number, had rallied and again beat back the invasion. But despite the successful defense of Earth by the Allied Nations Forces and the monstrous space expedition that had reportedly destroyed the Martians and their warlike civilization, the question in everyone's mind was, "What else is out there?"

These were my thoughts as I looked down on Baker Street from the front window of 221B. As usual, my reflections were interrupted by the voice of my godfather, Sherlock Holmes.

"It is they who should fear us, Jane. Now that we have access to their technology it will not be long before the people of Earth begin to travel to the stars. And when one considers how the indigenous people of Africa and the Americas were treated and the subjugation of the Indian subcontinent and parts of the Orient … as I said, whoever is out there should fear humanity. There are times I wonder if, having studied us, these so-called Martians were engaged in proactive self-defense.

"But you did not leave your lodgings in Praed Street to discuss the shape and fate of the world. Tell me of Fantômas."

I shrugged. "Not too much to relate, Uncle. Inspector Wiggins had told me about crimes that were reported to have been committed by well-known and respected citizens of London, all of whom denied any involvement but who could not or would not provide an alibi. The villain made the mistake of impersonating someone whose whereabouts were known to me."

"And that would be?"

"William Scott Adler."

I was well aware of Sherlock Holmes's past relationship with William's mother, the late Irene Adler, the one whom he always referred to as "the woman." Not wanting to know, I never inquired as to the extent of that relationship. Not even after William and I became intimate.

"And how was it you knew the whereabouts of the real Adler?"

"I'd rather not say," I replied but I'm afraid that my blushes gave me away.

Sherlock Holmes knows many things, and there are some things he chooses not to know or pretends not to. The extent of my relationship with William was one of them.

"And from that and the crime reports you deduced the heretofore unknown presence of Fantômas in this city. So with Adler safely out the way, presumably under the protection of my Praed Street colleague, you set a trap for his imposter. The fool should have stayed in France. Very good, Jane. Your father would have been proud of you."

Which was my godfather's way of telling me that *he* was proud of me.

You called Mycroft?" he asked.

"Of course."

"Good, he likes to be kept aware of this. Even now he is no doubt trying to determine how to use this criminal."

Holmes then handed me a telegraph that read, "Thornfax Manor is haunted. Come at once. Sir Thomas Clifford."

My godfather's view on the supernatural was "No ghosts need apply." This despite the fact that he had had dealings with a shape-shifting wolf on the Moors of Devon, a mummy that had escaped from the British Museum, a certain Transylvanian count (now a king), and had once been hired by Victor Frankenstein's creation to find what he believed to be his son. If these were possible, not to mention monsters from Mars, why not ghosts?

"The others may all have rational explanations, Jane," he had replied when I once asked him. "But for one's spirit to remain after death, unlikely."

"Says the man who came back from the Abyss."

"I was never dead. Your father merely thought I was."

Given his views on the matter, I was certain that my uncle would be anxious to investigate what natural agency was impersonating specters this time. He took great delight in unmasking criminals who disguised themselves as spirits to cover their crimes and several times had partnered with the American escapologist Houdini to expose those charlatans who preyed on the gullible.

"So when do you leave?" I asked him.

"I don't. It is not a good time for me to be away from London. Too many criminals are taking advantage of the unsettled conditions. In addition, my help has been requested in preparing for the next war. That maniac in Germany has already annexed Austria and parts of Czechoslovakia and is preparing to invade Poland."

"Can he be stopped?"

"He could, but Chamberlain has not the talent nor the inclination to do so. He, like so many in this country, is war weary. Unfortunately, Hitler and his National Socialists are not. Trust me, Jane, as I told you before, there will soon be another war.

"So I will not be able to lay the Thornfax Ghost, or whatever it is. Would you be available?"

"Things at the School of Medicine are quiet right now. I think I can be spared for a few days. Unless it turns out to be a real ghost."

That got me a snort of derision from my Uncle Sherlock. "Really, Jane."

4

Despite having had telephone service installed at Baker Street, Sherlock Holmes insisted on doing business by telegraph.

"Not everyone is on the line, Jane," he had explained. "And telegrams avoid the useless niceties that people seem to insist on when they use Mr. Bell's invention."

"I thought Elisha Gray had invented the telephone."

To this, my godfather had waved his hand, his way of dismissing what he regarded as a pointless argument.

Holmes sent Sir Thomas a return telegram stating that he would not be able to investigate but was instead sending his partner who would be arriving the next day. I spent that evening in my Praed Street apartment reviewing all that I knew about ghost hunting and considering what equipment I would need.

During what I regard as my apprenticeship as a detective, I spent time with investigators other than my uncle. I learned from Doctor Thorndyke, Max Carrados, and Martin Hewitt, and worked with Lady Molly of the Yard. I also hunted spirits with Thomas Carnacki and his chief rival Kelvin Meares.

It was thanks to the latter pair that I felt well-equipped to discover whatever was troubling Sir Thomas and his family.

Thornfax Manor had been the ancestral home of Lord Robert Capell. Lord Robert had been killed in a brave but ill-advised assault on a Martian Tripod during the second of the Martian Wars. He died without heirs or issue and the estate was purchased by Sir Thomas Clifford, who had been knighted for his efforts in the same campaign. Rumor had it that it was his wife Abigail who had insisted that her husband acquire the estate, in the mistaken belief that Lord Robert's title would devolve to its owner.

Driving a hired car, I arrived at Thornfax late the following morning. After I had given the servants instructions for the storing of my equipment, Sir Thomas and Lady Abigail greeted me and introduced me to their children, twins Amelia and Charles and their younger sister Dorothy.

I introduced myself adding, "Sherlock Holmes sends his regrets that matters of state prevented him from coming, I shall do my best to find the cause of the disturbance and, if possible, put an end to it."

"How would you like to begin, Doctor Watson?" Sir Thomas asked.

Before I could reply, young Dorothy asked, "I thought Doctor Watson was a man."

Lady Abigail quickly tried to hush her daughter but instead I replied, "That Doctor Watson was my father. It is because of him that I became a physician. He helped train me in medicine even as Sherlock Holmes trained me in, well, other things."

As I spoke to the young girl I studied her–age about ten or eleven whereas her siblings were a few years older. Her eyes were her best feature, bright and inquisitive, and I had no doubt that she was studying me even as I studied her. Somewhere in her room would be found copies of the Strand.

"I would like to be a doctor when I grow up."

"It takes a lot of hard work and rigorous study, so attend your lessons and maybe one day there will be a place for you at the London School of Medicine for Women. But for now, why don't you finish that chocolate cake you were eating before my arrival?"

Frosting at one corner of her mouth, a few strays crumbs on her collar. Dorothy's eyes widened at my deduction. With a "Yes, Ma'am. I mean, Doctor," the child ran off without waiting to be dismissed.

Mother and Father looked amused. The twins looked bored. "I think you have an admirer, Doctor," Sir Thomas said.

"It's those magazines and books you let her read," jokingly chided his wife. Then to me, she said, "I'll have a girl show you to your rooms. Then after dinner we can discuss how you wish to proceed with this ghost."

"I would like to start with the household staff," I told Sir Thomas and Lady Abigail after the evening meal. "Servants ofttimes see more than they say and yours might be able to shed some light on the matters that are troubling you. Speaking of which, how has this haunting manifested itself?"

Sit Thomas was hesitant to answer, so Lady Abigail spoke up.

"Strange noises, and not just at night. Several times both Thomas and I would be in one room and hear what we thought was someone in another but on investigating we found no one there. When asked, some of the servants reported similar occurrences. We often find doors ajar and drawers left open and sometimes things left in one place are found somewhere else."

"And, of course, there are noises in the night as if someone were walking around," Sir Thomas added. "And some of the servants reported whistling."

"Any recognizable tune?"

"None that they could identify."

"Are these phenomena limited to one floor or a particular part of the house?"

Both the Cliffords shook their heads. "They are as likely to be on the upper floors as on the ground floor," Sir Thomas said.

"Any priests' holes, servant passages, or other places that could conceal a person?"

"We, that is, Abigail thought of that and insisted we conduct a search. Some of the servants were retained after Lord Robert's death and none of them knew of any secret panels or passages."

I have some measuring to do, I thought. Just because secret places were not uncovered did not mean they weren't there.

"As far as you know, have any murders, suicides, or unexplained deaths or disappearances occurred in the house or on the grounds."

"All I know about the history of Thornfax Manor," Sir Thomas replied, "is from the portraits that were left hanging in the Great Hall. Names and faces, dates of births and deaths. That's all. If I had something with which to replace them or there was surviving family to whom I could give them, I would. Until then, they'll stay where they are. I suppose there are chronicles of the Capells in the library, the books there came with the house, but I haven't had time to read them. Feel free to look through them yourself."

I thought that I might have to, unless a certain inquisitive girl has already done so. The footsteps in the night might be young

Dorothy sneaking down to read books otherwise forbidden to her.

That was enough for one evening. I thanked Sir Thomas and Lady Abigail for their help. They thanked me for taking the time to help them and they retired for the night.

5

I spent that night alone in the dark of the Great Hall, surrounded by portraits of the dead. I sat and listened, alert for noises and footsteps. No noises save for those common to houses of the size of Thornfax Manor.

Before she retired, I took the opportunity to speak with Dorothy. She confessed to borrowing from the library from time to time but never at night and always with the permission of one of her parents. However, she had not bothered with any of the Capell family chronicles.

"So you would know nothing of any … unfortunate occurrences in the Capell family's past that might lead to a haunting?" I had asked her.

She said that she did not but from the gleam in her eye I was sure that she would soon act to correct this lack of knowledge should she find any such chronicles.

When working with Sherlock Holmes it was not uncommon to spend long hours sitting quietly in the dark. My godfather liked to lay traps and so we would wait, he with his leaded stick and my father or me with the Webley revolver; bullseye lanterns and later electric torches at the ready to expose the malefactor who always turned out to be the one Holmes suspected from the first.

(Except the one time when it was a pair of lovers who thought that the abandoned shed would be a perfect place for a tryst. But the less said about that "adventure" the better.)

When I heard the clocks strike two in the morning, I decided that if I were to question the servants in the morning and conduct my own search of the house and grounds, I would need some sleep. But before I went up to my rooms, I took the time to examine the portraits of the Capell family.

Or, rather, half of the family. As was the custom of the times, there were no portraits of the Capell women, just several generations of the "Lords" of the Manor and their sons and heirs. As family members do, all of them looked much the same–strong chins, Roman noses, brown hair, and dark eyes. However, there were some with white hair, pale skin, and light eyes, evidence that albinism ran in the family. The portraits were as Sir Thomas had described–name and faces, dates of births and deaths. *What did you expect, Jane*, I asked myself, *captions that read "killed by a jealous husband" or "hung as a traitor?"*

6

Morning came too early. I was awakened by the sun coming through my window and managed to rouse myself in time for breakfast. After that, I interviewed the staff. They told much the same story as had the Cliffords–things moved, doors and drawers found ajar or opened, unexplained footsteps and noises.

Four of the servants had been part of the Capell household–the butler, the cook, an upstairs maid, and the groundskeeper. After receiving assurances that the strange occurrences were not pranks being played on the new owners, I asked them what they knew of the family history. From what they told me, it seemed that the Capells may have been the most boring family in the history of the Isles–no murders, no family curses, no other-side-of-the-blanket births, no betrayals of king or country.

"There was one thing," the cook, Mrs. Payton, said. "Lord Robert's sister Constance, may she rest in peace, had three children, all sons. Two were lost in the Great War. The other, well, he was an odd one. He was named Thomas, like the current Master, and he was one of the pale ones, like in the pictures. One day he just left. We never saw him again. Broke his parents' heart he did."

"Did Lord Robert's sister and her family live here at Thornfax?"

"As it did so many others, the flu took his sister. But his brother-in-law and his nephews lived here. With the master not likely to have children of his own, it was understood that one of the nephews would inherit."

"What of Constance's husband?"

"He was a captain in the war. He died alongside his remaining two sons. Their deaths ended the Capell line."

After a suitable pause in which we remembered the dead of several wars, I asked Mrs. Payton if she had seen any signs of a ghost.

"If I had seen a ghost I would not be here, would I, Doctor? But there have been some strange goings on." She told me of noises, "knockings about" as she put it, and things being moved.

"Funny," she said, "one of my best knives disappeared from the kitchen. Sally found it in one of the upstairs bedrooms. And from time to time, food's gone missing. But that could be someone sneaking a treat." She shrugged. "Nothing to worry about I suppose."

After speaking to Mrs. Payton, I walked up to the bedroom she had mentioned. There was no damage to the room's door. I had not expected any, the rooms in Thornfax locked only from the inside. The room had a mustiness from not having been in use. Inside it were a poorly made up bed, a washstand, a dresser, a writing desk, and a heavy wardrobe. The drawer of the desk had a lock, as did the wardrobe. Taking out my glass, I examined them both and found minute scratches around the lock on the desk drawer. *Curious*, I thought. Opening the drawer, I found it empty. Had there been anything in there it was gone now.

I went back down to the kitchen.

"Mrs. Payton, if you know, the room in which your knife was found, whose was it?"

She thought for a moment or two, then, "Let's see, it was some time back. Lord Robert's grandfather I believe. There were a lot of them, seven, no eight in all, and they all lived, thank the Lord. Of course, Lady Capell was done worn out by the time the last arrived. I had just arrived, working in the kitchen and anywhere else I was needed. That room …" She closed her eyes and thought back to times past, her fingers working as if trying to place each child in its proper room. Finally, "That would have been young Alexander's."

"And what happened to him?"

The cook shrugged. "He was a middle son, neither the heir nor the spare. The army, the clergy, maybe government service. Who can say? Is it important?"

"No, Mrs. Payton. Just wondering why it was in that room the knife was found."

"Had to be somewhere, Doctor. Why would a ghost need a knife anyway?"

That was the same question I had asked myself, both when the cook first told me of the knife, when I found the scratches, and as I was measuring rooms and hallways and taking note of windows both inside and out, making sure that all matched up and there was no possibility of secret chambers, hidden rooms or, thinking back to the capture of Fantômas, trapdoors leading to spaces between floors. If nothing else, my work that day would provide Sit Thomas with the means of creating a fine architectural drawing of his new estate.

7

"Any progress, Doctor?" Lady Abigail asked during dinner. Before answering I quickly glanced at Dorothy who subtly shook her head. I then shook mine and replied, "Nothing toward finding the source of the disturbance. I spent the day eliminating some possibilities. As for tonight, I would ask that the household remain on the upper floors until morning. I have some tests I wish to conduct and any mortal presence might disturb the spirits." I said this last with a smile. Sir Thomas said that he would give the necessary orders.

I spent the evening with the family, entertaining them by recounting some of the adventures of Sherlock Holmes that my father had not chronicled in the Strand.

"What of the giant rat of Sumatra?" Dorothy asked.

"The world is still not ready for that story, I'm afraid." (From what my father had told me, it never will be. Let me just say that the Martians may not have been Earth's first otherworldly visitors.)

When it was time to retire, I excused myself and went back to the Great Hall. I was curious to see what young Thomas Capell looked like. Before I found him, however …

"Doctor Watson?"

I turned to see Amelia Clifford.

"Yes, Miss Clifford?"

"I was wondering. Do you see patients or do you just assist Mr. Holmes?"

"I am a physician first and assist Holmes when I can. Why?"

I suspected what was coming. It would not be the first time.

"Could you, would you see my sister and me as regular patients. I think we would be more comfortable being examined by a woman. And we both have questions about …"

"I understand, Miss Clifford. Before I depart, I shall give you both my home and professional phone numbers. Have your mother call and we can set up appointments for all three of you at the

London School of Medicine for Women. Is there anything else?"

I sensed that there was and I was correct.

"I think I saw the ghost."

Interesting. "Please, Miss Clifford, continue."

"It was about a week ago. Charles and my father were in the study going over the estate accounts. There was a storm. I was at the window in my room watching the rain. I thought I saw a man. It looked like a man, or rather, the rain was in the shape of a man. I watched it as best as I could. It seemed to be walking toward the side porch."

"And when it reached the porch?"

Amelia shook her head. "The raindrops seemed to disperse and there was nothing. And yes, I did go out the next day and look for shoeprints. My sister is not the only one who reads the Strand. But the rain was too heavy and had washed away any that were there. There was, however, mud on the porch."

Curiouser and curiouser. "Thank you, Miss Clifford, that is a great help. And I will be looking forward to your call about that other matter."

"Thank you, Doctor."

Alone with my thoughts and faces from the past, I found the portrait of Alexander Capell. Like his grandnephew Thomas, he too was a "pale one," an albino.

Coincidences happen. But in both my medical practice and my work with Sherlock Holmes, I have learned, well, not to distrust them but to heed them, as if the universe were drawing my attention to something. Of course, my godfather scoffed at this when I told him.

I studied the portrait and noticed that Alexander wore a ring on the index finger of his right hand. None of his brothers or his father did. Nor did any of the Capells save for the albinos. Taking out my ever-present glass, I examined the rings they wore, or rather, the ring, for they were all the same one.

A theory had begun to form, admittedly an improbable one, but a theory nonetheless. It was one I could work on while I was preparing to eliminate the impossible.

8

As I said, I had studied spirit detection under Carnacki and Meares. During my separate studies with them, they had both detected and produced manifestations, portals to other worlds rather than afterlives, and similar phenomena. But neither had found indisputable proof that there was life after death or that said life could return to this world in spirit form.

Meares took a more scientific approach than did Carnacki and it was his methods that I intended to follow that night. I had brought with me three magnetophon recorders and concealed them in areas where they would be most likely to capture any noises that occurred during the night. In those areas most likely to be trodden upon I sprinkled theft powder. (I would have to make apologies to the maids who would have some serious hoovering to do in the morning.) I also strung thin cords to which I had tied bells across doorways so that the breaking of the cords would cause the bells to ring.

My traps laid, I went up to my rooms, accompanied by a book I had borrowed from the manor's library. one written by Mr. Wells, the foremost chronicler of the First Martian War.

I lay awake all night, trying to read my so-called novel but mostly listening for sounds from below. Did I hear the tinkle of a bell? Was that a muffled oath? If so, did the recorder capture it? Would the "spirit" even appear given my presence in the house? And what percentage of the book I was reading was factual and how much was fictional?

9

Needing darkness for part of my investigation, I left my room an hour before dawn. This was the test. Had my instructions to Sir Thomas been overheard? If so, then my efforts of the previous night had been wasted. Or perhaps my quarry was avoiding me, ascribing to me powers of detection beyond those of mortal investigators, enhanced hearing or spectral vision like those brightly costumed heroes in American comic books. As for heightened senses, that was what the magnetophons and other devices were for.

As I left my room I carried a Byler Lamp which emitted ultraviolet light that would show me any disturbance in the thief powder.

There was faint luminescence at the tops of the stairs and maybe one or steps beyond it. It seemed to be heading down the hall toward the bedrooms. The poorly made bed in the room in which Mrs. Payton's knife was found. Sherlock Holmes would not have missed that. I suppressed the urge to rush into that room to see if the "ghost" was there, then realized that he could be there or in any of the others and I would not see him in any of them.

As I had expected, my quarry had avoided the cords with the bells. My godfather had taught me that when laying a trap, lay two, making sure that the first was easy to find and avoid.

What the intruder did not avoid was the theft powder. The black light of the Byler Lamp revealed footprints throughout the ground floor in rooms where there had not been any previous disturbance reported.

Thanks to my observations on the first floor, I had no fear of being watched or overheard. The ghost, I believed, was at bay for now.

Knowing that the servants would soon be awake to begin to prepare for the day, I carried the magnetophons up to my room. None of them were able to record more than thirty minutes of sound and I listened first to one, then another, hearing, if that is the proper word, nothing but the silence of the night. It was on the reel of the third device that I heard a faint noise that sounded like quiet laughter. This was followed by a whispered, "Nice try." Then came a low whistling.

It was off-key and barely audible. From what I could make out, it sounded like a song I had heard over the radio but I could not place it.

I had him and yet I did not. Not knowing when he might be watching or listening, I would have to proceed very carefully. It would not do for him to overhear my plans because I did not wish him to go away.

The next morning after breakfast, I announced plans to go into town. "I wish to consult with Sherlock Holmes and give him a progress report. Then I'll need to call the British Museum."

"So there has been progress?" Sir Thomas asked hopefully.

"Some, I believe. I'll know more after speaking with Holmes."

The looks given me by Sir Thomas and Lady Abigail indicated that they were losing faith in my abilities, faith which I hoped to restore soon.

The manor was on the telephone and before I departed, I had a whispered conversation with the butler and learned the number.

"I will be calling from town as soon as I can. Make certain that Sir Thomas is available to receive it."

Forty minutes later I rang the manor. When Sir Thomas came on I quickly said, "Do not say my name, Sir Thomas. Your 'ghost' is quite real and I do not want to chance your being overheard. Write down these instructions and if they are carried out there is a good chance that this matter can be resolved tonight."

For the midday meal Mrs. Payton had laid a cold buffet from which we served ourselves. Was *he* there, silently watching us? How many times previously had he done so, all the while wishing that he could join in?

"Sir Thomas," I asked, "from whom did you purchase Thornfax Manor?"

"From a distant relation of Lord Robert. She lives in the American Midwest and had no desire to come to Britain, not even to settle the estate."

"Were the contents of the house included with the sale?"

"Yes, they were, not that I've been able to go through them all."

"Was there any jewelry?"

"If so, my wife would have found it. Abigail?"

"I believe so, Thomas. I'll try to remember where it might be. Are you looking for any particular piece, Doctor?"

"As I was looking at the portraits of the Capells in the Great Hall I noticed that some wore a certain ring. I was wondering if it were included along with the other jewelry or if Thomas Capell had taken it with him when he disappeared."

The Clifford children suddenly became interested.

"Is it precious?" Charles asked.

"Or magical or cursed?" Dorothy added hopefully.

"Is it that this ghost is a burglar looking for the Capell treasure? Amelia wanted to know."

"Could it be Raffles, Doctor?"

"It could be *a* raffles, Dorothy," I said. "The real Raffles gave his life for his country in the Boer War. But to answer your questions, I described the ring to an expert in Greek Antiquities who said that it might be The Ring of Gyges which, if so, would make it of great historical interest."

My talking with an antiquities expert was a lie. The ring, however, was something I remembered from the time my father and godfather had assisted an Oxford Professor of the English Language with the recovery of his translation of Beowulf. After the manuscript had been found, the four of us sat discussing language, fantasy as literature, and magic. It was during the discussion of the latter that The Ring of Gyges was mentioned. I remember thinking how useful such a ring would be to an investigator.

Using a Langley Bolometer, I spent the afternoon and early evening inspecting the room of the upper floors for heat signatures. I did not expect to find any, but if I had it would have made that night's charade unnecessary. I did, however, observe several more unmade beds.

During dinner, I wanted to use the bolometer to see if we

were being observed but dared not. All I could do was hope he was listening.

"Doctor Watson," Lady Clifford said, "I found the chest which holds the Capell jewels, such as they are. I suspect that most of them were sold for the war effort and that what remains had of more of a sentimental value."

She handed me a small jewel box. I thanked her and placed the box in my bag. "I'll look these over tonight in my room. For now, I think I'll inspect the ground floor rooms."

As I used the bolometer (without success), I was conscious of the possibility of being grabbed and attacked in an effort to seize my bag. *Let him*, I thought, confident of the skills in close-in fighting that a *baritisu* master had taught me. I ended my evening in the Great Hall. As I looked again at the portraits, I thought about my plans for the night. I wondered if Sherlock Holmes, as he sat in the darkness waiting for events to unfold, ever worried about or questioned his course of action. Had he observed all or was there something he had missed? Had he made the right deductions from what he observed? Had some slight error at the beginning caused his investigation to go off course?

Probably not, for he was Sherlock Holmes. And even if he had worried about such things, being Sherlock Holmes he would likely not admit it.

It was getting dark. There was no moon that night. It was time to put aside all doubts and capture a ghost.

As I slowly ascended the stairs to the first floor, I kept one hand firmly on the banister and the other tightly gripping my bag, my body prepared against any attempt to push me down the steps. None came. When I arrived at my room I noticed that the small piece of paper that I had subtly placed in the latch jam was now on the floor. I then saw that the hairs I had left on the doorknob were gone.

I had left the light on. I looked around the room and, seeing nothing, threw my bag on the bed, hopefully distracting him.

Pausing to control my breathing, I switched the light off, putting the room in darkness and giving myself the advantage.

Neither of us could see the other. He could not escape through the door, for I was blocking it. He could not leave by the window. Even if it were not locked, it could not be opened thanks to the two small wedges I placed between the sashes.

With my eyes closed tightly, I stood in the dark watching and listening. He had, by necessity, learned to move stealthily so as not to be detected. Was he moving closer to me, preparing to strike me, push me aside, and escape through the hall and down the stairs? Or was he edging closer and closer to the bag on the bed and the precious treasure inside it?

I judged five minutes or more had passed and decided it was time to act. Being a doctor, I knew of those people known as albinos. I knew that they were burned badly by the sun. I knew that their eyes were very sensitive to light, my opponent's even more so. There was a dresser to my left. Keeping my eyes shut, I picked up the torch I had left there. Flicking it on, I swept the room with its powerful beam.

There was a cry of pain and I rushed toward it. Encountering his body, I hit him twice in the abdomen then struck his neck in such a way that he fell unconscious.

Unable to see him, I used my hands and fingers to examine him. His pulse was steady, his breathing sounded normal, and I could feel no damage to his face or upper body. All seem fine except … I checked his facial features again. *Even more curiouser.*

Leaving him on the floor, I switched the light back on. Shielding my eyes, I looked over to where he had fallen. As I had expected, I did not see him. That did not stop me from sitting him up, binding him with strong rope, and subjecting him to a few investigative techniques.

That was one mystery solved, the "ghost" was, as I had expected, an invisible man. Ghosts, after all, would not need to eat or sleep. Yet food was missing and beds were slept in.

The problem now was what to do with him.

My initial thought was to reveal him, so to speak, to the Cliffords. But the existence of such beings as vampires, werewolves, reanimations such as Adam Frankenstein, and invisible men was a closely guarded state secret. The world can barely handle the idea of aliens from space. Creatures of the Abyss (as Mycroft Holmes once described them) would be too much for it. Which is why H. G. Wells, following the examples of Stoker and Shelley, presented the story of Griffin as fiction rather than fact.

There was a moan from where my captive was laying. Looking over, I saw the ropes move as if he were trying to free himself.

"Don't struggle," I told him. "I was taught those knots by Houdini. If you struggle, they'll only get tighter." The ropes stopped moving.

"That is better, Mister Capell. It is Capell, isn't it? Thomas Capell? The last surviving member of a once-great family?"

"Er, yes." Capell's voice was rough and scratchy, as if he were not used to talking. Given his circumstances, I supposed he was not.

"Please be assured, Thomas, that I am not in the habit of entertaining naked men in my room, whether I can see them or not. I shall have to obtain some clothing for you. But first, how did you come to be in the state you are in?"

"I ... left, was afraid ... to fight. Man named Griffin ... found me. He was ... bandaged, said ... he needed my ... help."

As Capell spoke his speech came easier. Soon he was speaking normally, although his voice remained raspy.

"Griffin said that he needed my help, then he showed me why. Like me, he had been what my family called a pale one. Said he needed my help to become visible again. I thought maybe he knew about the ring, but instead, he attacked me and rendered me unconscious. Like you did."

I made no apologies. Naked or not, men who come into my room uninvited deserve whatever happens to them. (I will not speak of what happens to those I invite.)

"When I awoke I was strapped to an examination table. Griffin injected me with something and slowly I faded. Soon I was as much of a ghost as he. He explained his formula only truly works on pale ones. Others it kills, slowly and otherwise. After that, he tried various treatments on me. Some did nothing, some were painful. None of them restored me to visibility."

Even though I knew I was talking to a man, I must confess

there was a certain eeriness in conversing with a disembodied voice. "How did you escape?"

"I was as invisible to him as he to me. One day he let his guard down. I got free of my shackles, shed the clothes he had given me, and, well, disappeared. Then I came home."

"To search for the ring?"

"Not at first. Imagine returning home to find your family destroyed, your birthright gone, your home in the possession of strangers. At first, I thought to kill them. It would have been easy, either one at a time or all in one night. But despite those who would make it so," the ropes around Capell's wrists pointed to the nightstand where I had left Wells's book, "I am not a monster. Neither did I take advantage of my condition to spy on the women. I was raised a gentleman, Doctor Watson, and a gentleman I remain."

"I believe you. About the Ring of Gyges?"

"I do not know how it came into the family's possession, but it was only given to the pale ones such as I. It was said that the ring would keep us from fading. Alexander was the last one to wear it. After him, it was lost. I thought maybe I could find it and hopefully restore myself." There was a pause, then, "The ring is not in your bag, is it?"

"No, it's not," I admitted. "It was a trick, to trap you."

"Then I am lost, condemned by a madman and my own cowardice to be forever damned."

I then broke a rule. I told Capell of MI-7, the secret agency that protects Great Britain against extra-normal threats. "You could find a home there. You can serve your country and do honor to the memory of Lord Richard and your brothers."

There was a loud sigh then, "I don't seem to have any choice. I had thought that if the ring worked, I could file suit to reclaim the Manor but now ..."

"You wouldn't be able to appear in court."

There was still the matter of the Cliffords. As I have pointed out, telling them the truth about Thomas Capell was out of the question. There was only one other option.

Addressing Capell I said, "I have some preparations to make. I shall be back presently and we can put an end to this and start you on your new life."

"As you seem to be my only hope I have no choice. And you have my word that I will not try to escape."

Despite his choices being between MI-7 or a life of misery, I did not know how good his word was. I left him bound.

The activities in my room had attracted attention. Waiting outside my door were the butler, the upstairs maid, Sir Thomas, and, bless her inquisitive heart, Dorothy. She was the one who asked, "Is everything all right, Doctor Watson?"

"Yes, everything is fine. Now. One cannot confront a ghost without some noise."

"Then it was a ghost?" Sir Thomas asked. And at my nod, "Is it there now? What's to be done?"

"There is presently no ghost in my room," I said truthfully. "As to what may be done, I know the hour is late but that will work in our favor. Please instruct your staff to remain in their rooms and gather your family in the dining room. I will join you shortly."

After an incident in Bancroft, my godfather gave me a telephone number to use if I needed help. I called it that night.

The phone on the other end rang several times before, "Yes, what is it?"

"It's Jane, Uncle Mycroft."

"How many times have I told you not to call me that, Doctor? And why are telephoning me in the middle of the night?"

"Because I do not know how to get in contact with Sir Denis Nayland Smith. And I believe that you have been acting in his stead since his old nemesis has returned."

"For now. That may change very soon. What do you have?"

I told Mycroft of the invisible man and his failed quest for the ring.

"That college professor Sherlock helped donated that ring to the British Museum," he said. "And your prisoner would be of interest to the ministry. When and where can he be produced?"

I told Mycroft where to meet us and what to expect. My phone call complete, I went first to my room. I gave my captive his instructions then dragged him to the top of the stairs where I bound him to the top railing. I then descended to the dining room where I found the Capell family.

They had not bothered to dress but instead were dressed in their nightclothes and robes. I had them pull the chairs out from the table and arrange them in a circle. Once we were seated I said, "Would everyone please join hands."

They did, Dorothy enthusiastically grasping mine while the others hesitantly completed the chain.

I began to chant in a mixture of Latin, Greek, and Old Gaelic using phrases and songs that Carnacki and Meares employed to call forth spirits, changing them just enough so as to avoid an accidental summons. After about five minutes, I judged the Cliffords suitably impressed. I then loudly cried out, "I seek the spirit of Thomas Capell. Thomas, are you with us?"

No answer and so I asked again. "Thomas Capell, are you with us?"

Than there came a sepulchral "Yes," seemingly from nowhere and everywhere. Dorothy's hand squeezed mine. Somehow, through her I felt her family members tense.

"Why do you haunt this house, Thomas? What do you want?"

"This was my home. I returned to seek the Ring of Gyges. Only that can free me."

"The ring is lost. It is not here."

"I sense that now."

"Then you must seek it elsewhere. Depart from this house and never return."

"Wait!"

The cry came from Dorothy who then said, "Mr. Capell, this was your home?"

"Yes, it was."

"Then you should not have to leave."

"Dorothy…" her father started to say but Dorothy continued. "No, Father, you and Mother have taught us to be fair. If Mr. Capell does not want to leave he should not have to."

This was unexpected. But before I could figure out what to do or say, Thomas replied,

"Thank you, Miss Clifford, but I feel myself being called to a higher purpose and so must leave."

"Then you must visit. We will leave a bell in the Great Hall. When you come ring it so that we know you are here and we will make you welcome."

"I thank you, and I may if it is permitted. But for now, farewell."

And so the Ghost of Thornfax Manor was exorcised.

10

The next morning, I woke early and placed my captive in my car before anyone woke. Should any look inside all they'd see were ropes and a set of keyless handcuffs as had been used on Fantômas. After that, I received the thanks of Sir Thomas and Lady Abigail (along with a sizable cheque for services rendered). With my car packed, and a naked, invisible man secure in the back seat, I drove away from Thornfax Manor.

I had not driven far, just enough to be out of sight of Thornfax Manor, when I was approached by several vehicles. I slowed then stopped as they blocked my way.

"What is this?" asked the man in the back.

"Surely, Griffin. You did not think that you fooled me. Now then, what have you done with the real Thomas Capell."

There came from the backseat a laugh that was part evil and part madness. "You'll never find his body."

From the lead car emerged Mycroft Holmes and, to my surprise, my godfather. Leaving Griffin behind I got out and joined them.

"Good day to you, Uncles."

Mycroft harrumphed. Holmes let out a rare laugh then said, "Very good, Jane. Well done. It was very clever of you to realize that one invisible man looks much like the other. What made you suspect?"

"When I examined him in my room, I noted that his facial features—nose, chin, the shape and size of his ears, did not match those of any of the Capells. Furthermore, he failed to correct me when I called his father Lord Richard rather than Lord Robert." I handed Mycroft a small bag. "Here is a blood sample I took from Griffin, along with a drinking glass that should bear his fingerprints. I assume you have records of his blood group and fingerprints. If so, that should confirm his identity."

"Excellent work, Jane. Would you not say so, Mycroft?"

"Satisfactory." This, from Mycroft Holmes, was high praise

indeed.

Relieved of my burden, I drove back to London alone. Switching on the car radio, I heard a band playing the song that Griffin had been tunelessly whistling. Finding it apt, I had no choice but to sing along.

Yesterday, upon the stair,
I met a man who wasn't there!
He wasn't there again today,
Oh how I wish he'd go away!

11

Interlude
1894–The Taking of Dracula

The moon was full that night, its reflected light casting eerie shadows and turning trees into sinister figures. This did not bother the man who had just scaled the solid stone wall that surrounded the estate. Dropping noiselessly to the ground, he easily made his way through the heavily wooded grounds until he came to the abbey itself.

In the moonlight, Carfax Abbey showed a glamor that did not exist by day. The night hid the decay, the ruin, and the neglect it had suffered over decades of abandonment. It had been hoped the new owner would return Carfax to its former glory, but he had preferred it as it was, its lifeless condition reflecting his own.

Slowly, carefully, the man approached the house. When he came close, he observed that the front door was ajar. Making his way around the side, he saw a patio, its paving cracked and overgrown with weeds. He considered and rejected the patio's French doors and continued his anti-clockwise tour around the building. One window conveniently opened, another with its glass broken out. Both accessible, neither seeming right or safe.

You are overthinking this. The voice in his head was that of his old friend, his only true friend, the man he wished was at his side that night. But the time for that had not yet come. *Soon* he told himself, *once this is over, once England is again safe.*

The back door, the servants' and tradesmen's entrance. Still intact, still locked. The man took out his dub keys, blackened against the moonlight, the ones the cracksman had left him. The third one worked, the lock yielding without a sound, the door opening without a creak of its hinges.

The man pushed the door open and was about to enter when

he realized what the lack of noise meant. He jumped back just as the heavy beam crashed down on where he would have been.

So much for the element of surprise, he thought. Suppressing the urge to inspect the portals he had bypassed to see if similar traps had been laid, or if his quarry had simply succeeded in duplicating his thought processes, the man moved into the house. With an air pistol in his right hand and a bullseye lantern in his left, he began his search for possibly the most dangerous creature he had ever faced.

His plan was to first search the second floor and work his way down through the first and the ground levels, ending in the cellar if need be. If he found nothing, then he would search the old family crypt, although he thought that too obvious. But given what had just happened, he thought that maybe the obvious was the best place to start.

But then he heard it, a phonograph playing a mournful tune. He followed the sound into the drawing-room, where he found the one he sought sitting quietly in a high-back chair, his eyes closed as he listened to the music.

"Listening to the music of the night, Count De Ville? Or do you prefer Monsieur Vladimir? Perhaps Voivode Tepes? Or Count Dracula?"

The count slowly opened his eyes, which seemed to reflect the yellow of the flames which burned in the fireplace. He stood and faced the man. Although dressed simply in trousers and an open-necked white shirt, the count still maintained a noble presence.

"Count Dracula will suffice. And how shall I address you, sir? Sigerson, or perhaps Allard, or do you prefer the name by which your public knows you–Sherlock Holmes?" When Holmes acknowledged this recognition with a nod, the count said, "Forgive my asking, but are you not supposed to be dead?"

"The same could be said of you, Count."

"*Touché*. Rest assured, Mr. Holmes, that I am alive, albeit in a different way than you, and with different needs, desires, and appetites. Just how did you find me?"

"Does it matter?"

"No, I do not suppose it does."

Ignoring the pistol in Holmes's hand, the count walked over to the phonograph and turned it off. "By now," he said, "Harker and the other fools are in Europe chasing what they believe to be my last coffin. When they catch up to it, my *Romani* will make a pretense of protecting me, possibly killing one or more of them before fleeing. What, or rather who, the fools find when they open the coffin will look very much like me. They will kill this poor innocent, congratulate themselves on a job well done, then return in triumph to England. Where I will be waiting."

"And then what, Count?"

Dracula smiled, his canines sharp and white. "What do you think, Mr. Holmes?"

"I cannot allow that."

"You cannot prevent it. That weapon in your hand cannot harm me. I am faster and stronger than you. You are believed by all to be dead. Tonight that belief will become a ..."

The pistol in Holmes's hand coughed as a dart flew from it and lodged itself in Dracula's exposed neck.

"What ..." asked the count as he felt a weakness come over him.

"A fast-acting paralytic agent, designed specifically to react with your particular body chemistry."

As Holmes spoke, Dracula fell to the floor. The detective continued talking. "Although you cannot move, you can hear me. So understand this, Count Dracula. However much you deserve death, there are those who believe that you have a part to play in future events. And so I have been instructed to let you live. When the drug wears off, you will find yourself back in the Carpathians. Remain there and claim your destiny. But be warned, should you return to England I will hunt you down. And once I find you, there will be the stake, the knife, and the fire."

Fighting against the drug and losing, Dracula nodded his understanding and surrender. Then he lapsed into unconsciousness.

When he awoke, Dracula was, as Holmes had promised, in his castle in the Carpathian Mountains. The castle had been ransacked, his *Romani* guards killed, his brides slaughtered or fled. He did not dwell on this loss very long. He was a soldier and understood defeat.

It, like life itself, was something to be overcome. He would rebuild and, as the detective had advised, claim his destiny. But for now, he was tired and hungry. *Tonight*, he thought, *I need to hunt and feed. Tomorrow*, he promised himself, *I will begin, for tomorrow is another night.*

12

The Affair at Dracula's Castle

From the diary of Jane Watson
The great airship the *Carpathia* slowly lifted off from the Harmondsworth Aerodrome in Heathrow. From the outside, it looked very much like the Zeppelins of the 1930s whose era ended with the explosion of *The Hindenburg*. But the *Carpathia* was not a hydrogen-filled deathtrap. Instead, it used the Martian technology the Kingdom of Transylvania had acquired at the end of the Second Invasion. It was silent and safe but it was only now, three years after the disaster at Lakehurst, New Jersey, that the public was beginning to trust this mode of travel.

The *Carpathia* was one of four airships owned and operated by Transylvania. It served Europe and North Africa. Its sister ships, the *Romani*, the *Justina*, and the *Ilona*, served North America, South America, and Asia, respectively.

Barely feeling the takeoff, I watched from my cabin's large window as the ground slowly fell away from me. It was not my first time in the air, although the *Carpathia* was considerably more comfortable than the biplanes I had flown when I was fourteen.

We were fifteen minutes in the air when the captain's voice came over the loudspeaker to announce, in Romanian, Hungarian, Russian, German, and finally English, that we would be landing at the Cluj-Napoca Aerodrome in six hours. (Travel by airship is comfortable but slow.)

Good, I thought, *that will give me time to review the situation.*

13

A few days before, I was with Sherlock Holmes in his Baker Street flat. He had just taken out his syringe and the solution he had once told my father was "Cocaine, a seven percent solution." It was not. Instead it was a combination of apian Royal Jelly mixed with a highly diluted solution of an "elixir of life" supposedly discovered by the notorious Victor Frankenstein. I'm not sure that my father would have approved of this any more than he did with the idea of his friend taking recreational stimulants.

As a physician myself, I certainly did not approve of my godfather taking such an elixir, particularly one developed by the infamous Frankenstein. But Holmes showed me the notes he had taken from Frankenstein's journals, the writings of Sir Isaac Newton that supported those notes, and his own research. The science appeared sound and he himself was living proof. Although at the time of this writing Sherlock Holmes was over eighty, he had the appearance and vitality of a man in his early sixties. So convincing was his evidence, that after my father died in 1929, I too began taking the injections and now appear to be at least a decade younger than my true age.

We injected each other and after the mild euphoria had passed, he asked me to again recount how I captured Griffin, the Invisible Man.

"Why, Uncle, are you planning to write up my adventures for The Strand?"

"No, Jane. I doubt if I could do you as much justice as your late father did me. It's just that …"

Whatever he was going to say was interrupted by the telephone. Holmes disliked having one but acknowledged its necessity.

"Holmes here … Yes, I see. Very well, Brother, I will see you shortly … Yes, she's here … Very well, I shall bring her along."

"How is Uncle Mycroft?"

"You know, Jane, he hates it when you call him that."

"I know."

"You saw him at the end of the Thornfax Manor Affair. My brother is doing well for a man in his nineties but his age is catching up to him. And yet he refuses to consult you or any other physician."

"Why does he want to see us?"

"We will discover that at the Diogenes Club."

The Diogenes Club began as a club for "unclubbable men," or so wrote my father. It was also the secret, and now not so secret, center for what became the British Secret Service, code name MI-6. Very few knew that its basement and sub-basements housed another agency, MI-7, which protected the Realm against monsters and unworldly threats.

When we arrived, we were immediately led to Mycroft's first-floor office by Sir Miles. The man who at times *was* the British Government did not look well. I had seen him only briefly in the affair of Thornfax Manor. Now I observed that he no longer filled out his specially made chair, one designed to support a quarter of a ton, and in the light of the electric lamps which lit the room he seemed pale.

"Spare me your diagnoses, Doctor Watson," he growled before either my uncle or I could speak. "I am fully aware of my condition and even were you to give me medical advice it is unlikely I would follow it. Life without good food, good wine, and good cigars is not worth living." Turning to his brother he said, "And no, Sherlock, I have no wish to extend my given lifespan artificially."

"Benson the murderer was hung yesterday," remarked my godfather. "He seems a fine specimen. If you can lay hold of the Swiss doctor he could replace Benson's brain with yours, allowing you to live, well, forever."

"Pfui," Mycroft huffed at his brother's jest. "And need I remind you that Victor Frankenstein is not and never was a doctor."

Mycroft invited us to sit then, "Speaking of doctors, Sir Denis Nayland Smith has once again gone off in pursuit of the Chinese Doctor, who may or not be a doctor and is probably not even Chinese. But the point is that he is no longer in charge of MI-7. A new head has been appointed."

Lifting the receiver of this phone, he spoke into it. "Bring her in, Sir Miles." He then turned to his brother. "Now, Sherlock, I'll need you to be calm. This decision has been made at the highest level and there's nothing to be done about it."

"My dear brother, since when have you seen me other than calm and rationa ..."

The door opened and Mycroft's assistant led in an attractive red-haired woman who was seemingly in her mid-twenties but who, in reality, was much older. Like me, she was dressed in the fashion of the times, having given up the male attire she had previously preferred.

"Sherlock, Doctor Watson, I believe you both know Lady Katherine Barnaby."

We did. Thanks to Victor Frankenstein, the body of Katherine Barnaby housed the brain of my godfather's old nemesis Professor James Moriarty. Upon her return from the Abyss, Barnaby had at first resumed her criminal ways, becoming, as Holmes had put it, the "Josephine of Crime." However, during the Great War and the First Martian Invasion she began working with the government rather than against it. For her efforts both during and after these conflicts, Lady Barnaby was awarded a full pardon for her crimes as well as the Most Excellent Order of the British Empire.

(For the record, Sherlock Holmes has several times been offered this honor and more besides. Each time he has respectfully declined. When my father asked once asked him why Holmes replied, "I am Sherlock Holmes, and that is enough for me.")

Despite her pardon and honors, Holmes had never forgiven Lady Barnaby (nee Moriarty) for her crimes. As he stood to greet her, only I (and possibly Mycroft) could see the anger inside him. With his face almost as red as her hair, he gave her the slightest of bows and said, "My Lady."

Smiling, Lady Barnaby returned his bow then asked, "M, have you told him of the situation?"

"No, K, I have not."

"Then let us begin."

Sitting to one side of Mycroft's desk, Lady Barnaby addressed us.

"My section recently received a communiqué from our consulate in Transylvania. It was addressed to 'Sherlock Holmes and Doctor Jane Watson.' To be brief, there has been a murder at Castle Dracula and King Vlad wishes you to solve it."

There was a slight pause to allow both Holmes and me to take this in. Finally, my godfather said, "Please send my apologies to the Count and inform him that I am busy here in London and could not possibly leave at this time. Advise him that there are several competent investigators in Europe. Monsieur Poirot, for one. No wait, he will be busy in Belgium. Let us pray he gets out before it is too late. There is Joseph Muller of the Austrian Secret Police. He is almost as astute as Doctor Watson or myself and he does take private commissions."

Still smiling, Lady Barnaby interrupted my godfather saying, "Forgive me, Mr. Holmes, but King Vlad's message to you was that while he greatly respects, and here I quote, 'the only man to have beaten me' he does not wish to take you from London at this time." Here Lady Barnaby turned to me. "It is you, Doctor Watson, that he is requesting. King Vlad has promised you safe passage both going and returning on board the, again I quote, 'safest airship the world has ever seen.' He also guarantees your safety and well-being while you are his 'honored guest.'"

Surprised by this, I took time to think. Did I wish to travel across a land that was likely to be engulfed in war in a matter of months, if not weeks? Did I wish to visit a vampire's lair with the possibility I would be trapped there for the duration? And did I wish to confront the horrors and monsters I might encounter in that lair?

"I would prefer not to," I answered calmly.

Lady Barnaby and Mycroft looked at each other, their expressions indicating that they had expected my answer.

"We would like you to reconsider, Doctor," Mycroft said. "Transylvania is, for now, remaining neutral in the upcoming conflict. King Vlad's own statement was 'Make war all you wish but do not involve us or our country. Should you do so, it will be at your peril and to your regret.' We do not wish to do anything to have him reconsider this policy. In addition, assisting him in this matter may make him more amenable to the anti-fascist cause. "

"There is another reason, is there not, Brother?"

"Yes, there is, Sherlock. Doctor Watson, as his investigator, you will be given access to parts of Dracula's castle that no Englishman other than Jonathan Harker has ever seen. With your powers of observation, you can return with information that could prove useful should there be a need to act against him. And if that is not enough to convince you …"

Mycroft handed me an envelope. On seeing the royal seal, I did not need to open it to know its contents.

"For King and Country then, Uncle Mycroft."

For once, the elder Holmes smiled at my calling him that. "For King and Country, Niece."

"Jane, I do not think …"

Handing my godfather the envelope with the seal up, I said, "Uncle Sherlock, if you can look me in the eye and tell me that if this were addressed to you, you would refuse, then I shall remain in London."

"Damn it, Jane," he whispered so low that only I could hear him.

By now, Sir Miles had poured us all a drink, the finest from the Diogenes's cellar. Standing, we all raised our glasses.

Mycroft gave the toast. "For King and Country." We echoed him and then Holmes added, "And a safe journey there and back again."

As we left, I walked out with the newly appointed head of MI-7.

"Lady Barnaby …"

"Yes, Doctor Watson?"

"I wanted to ask you about Griffin. Have you had any problems in keeping the Invisible Man detained?"

She shook her head. "Not at all. Once he was in custody we painted his legs, arms, and face blue. The paint needs to be reapplied daily. His chest and abdomen we leave invisible so as to allow the Fellows of the Royal Society to study the processes of digestion and elimination."

"Interesting. If I may ask, is the, um, final product also invisible?"

"Fortunately, no. If you are interested in joining the Society, I can have you nominated for membership."

"I have applied, Lady Barnaby, but the Royal Society takes the word "Fellows" literally."

"Mmm, that will have to change. Despite my reformation, I am in touch with elements of my former life and I have knowledge that may help to change the minds of the committee members."

I suspected that by "in touch" she meant "I am still secretly running my criminal syndicate." However, all I said was, "How is Mrs. Stamford these days?"

At first, she looked surprised at my knowledge of her former(?) organization but then remembered who my godfather was and merely smiled and nodded. "Aging well, but still in command. But I, or rather, she will have to start looking for a successor. Might you be interested? I think you would do well as 'The Professor.'"

"Thank you, Lady Barnaby, but I prefer to, as the Americans say, 'wear the white hat.'"

Another smile. "I prefer gray myself. Anyway, good luck to you, Doctor Watson. We should meet again on your return."

"I look forward to it, Lady Barnaby."

And I did, in much the same way Holmes had looked forward to their meeting at the Reichenbach Falls.

We parted ways, the once and current Moriarty to her offices in the basement and I to the Strangers' Room to await Holmes.

14

With my needing time to prepare for my journey with an early flight the next day, our walk home was likely the last chance for Holmes and me to converse before my departure.

"Jane, I will not tell you to take care, for I know you will. Just as I know that you have all the skills needed to succeed in a case as difficult as this might be. Just, do not trust Dracula. He is handsome and charming but beneath his looks and charm, he is a creature from the Abyss who is not to be trusted. And may I add, neither is the so-called Lady Barnaby. She may appear to be an attractive young woman but her brain is that of a monster every bit as evil as Dracula."

After that, except for my godfather whispering, "I should have made sure he was dead," we walked in silence until Holmes said, "I almost forgot. Mycroft told me that the Ring of Gyges was stolen from the British Museum."

"Are you going to investigate?"

"The trail is cold but a simple case of burglary would make a nice change."

I told Holmes of how MI-7 was keeping track of Griffin. "So that's one suspect out of the way."

"Yes, but there is another."

We had come to our, hopefully temporary, parting of our ways. "The usual codes, Uncle?

"Yes, use Gibson's latest. For an American writer, he has quite a devious mind when it comes to ciphers. Now go, and God be with you, Jane."

"And you too, Uncle." He permitted me to kiss his cheek and then we parted.

15

*F*or *King and Country*, I reminded myself as the *Carpathia* cleared the Channel. As the French landscape unfolded beneath me, I imagined what it would be like within the year. Poland was being threatened and would fall as soon as Germany invaded. Then the allied nations would declare war, which means Belgium and France would quickly succumb, leaving England democracy's sole defender until the United States got into the war. I prayed that the Americans would not arrive too late.

Pushing these dark thoughts aside, I left my cabin and went to the main lounge in the forward part of the airship. The nose of the ship was made of an acrylic glass said to be much stronger than that currently being used commercially. As with the technology powering the *Carpathia*, this "glass" was rumored to be the result of Martian technology. Whatever its origin, its position in the very front of the ship gave the illusion of flying if one stood close to it.

"It is very much like the comic book *Übermensch,* is it not?" Someone behind me asked in German-accented English. I turned to see a man in his middle years who wore his suit like a uniform. It did not take great deductive skills to discern that he was a German military man trying to pass as a civilian. "To be flying in the air without fear, to be the strongest, to be the best. What do you think, Fräulein?"

As he said this last, he put his arm around my waist.

"I think that I will break your arm if you do not remove your arm this instant. Then I will test the strength of this window by trying to throw you through it."

He quickly withdrew his arm. Giving a light bow he said, "Forgive me, Fräulein. I had merely thought to be friendly."

I considered telling him in street German exactly what I thought he was doing but I decided it was best if he assumed that I did not speak his language. Instead, I looked at him as if I had accepted his apology.

"Allow me to introduce myself, Fräulein. I am Herr Joachim

Rosin."

I had seen Rosin at the aerodrome earlier. He was studying the *Carpathian*, admiring it in the way that a driver at LeMans would admire the new Bugatti. Now, up close, I noticed faint tan marks around his eyes, the kind one gets from wearing goggles regularly.

Rosin was no doubt expecting me to return the introduction. Instead, I asked, "Tell me, Herr Rosin, what was or is your rank in the Luftwaffe?"

The look on his face was one I had seen many times on the faces of police, clients, and my father, who never fully learned just how his friend, and later his daughter, did what we did. As Rosin stood there wondering, I said, "Allow me to introduce myself, Herr Rosin. I am Doctor Jane Watson."

Understanding replaced confusion. "I recognize your name. You are associated with Sherlock Holmes, are you not?" I admitted that I was. "And your travel to Transylvania, is it related to your medical profession, or are you representing Mister Holmes?"

As I was about to tell him that whatever business I was on was none of his, I heard, "Young lady, is the major here bothering you?"

The man coming to my unneeded aid was of medium height, in his sixties but looked older due to excess weight and the graying of whatever hair he had left.

"It is all right, Sir Nigel, Major Rosin and I were getting to know one another."

He paused for a moment then "Is that you, Jane? I'm sorry, I should say 'Doctor Watson' shouldn't I? Congratulations on that. Are you still associated with Holmes?"

He knew that I was. Holmes and I had assisted him when his daughter went missing. The suspected abduction turned out to have been an elopement.

Recalling that Sir Nigel was with His Majesty's Diplomatic Service and noting his familiarity with Rosin, I observed, "Make certain that you both remove your hats when presenting your credentials to King Vlad. Remember what happened to those Ottoman ambassadors."

With that, I left them, two men who seemed friendly enough to one another but who were soon fated by circumstances to be enemies.

There were others in the main lounge. A newly married couple (they looked only at each other when they weren't glancing at their bright, new wedding bands), three Anglican nuns possibly going to Transylvania to maybe convert its monsters. *Luck and God go with them*, I silently prayed. There were two men of business, arms merchants. If the opportunity arose I would play the innocent, learn what I could about them, and later report to Mycroft.

Then there was a man standing away from the forward window, carefully not watching the landscape but rather studying his fellow passengers. As I was, in turn, studying him, it was inevitable that our eyes would meet. He nodded, I smiled, and, after a moment's hesitation, he walked over to me.

He was tall, tan, and broad-shouldered, with heavy brows and a full, dark beard. His suit fit him well, or maybe he fit it well. Despite this, there was something of the savage about him. At first, I thought that he might be the Viscount from Africa about whom Burroughs had written, but he did not seem to be a man of the jungle. By the time he reached me I knew that I did not want to play the innocent with this man.

There was both French and German in his voice as he said, "My lady, please allow me to introduce myself. I am Frederick Morrow."

"And I am Doctor Jane Watson. I am pleased to meet you, Herr Morrow." I offered him my hand–to shake, not to kiss–and as he took it I could not help but notice that his ring finger was longer than his middle one. This coupled with the fact that his eyebrows met and there was a slight musky odor about him led me to a certain conclusion.

"Are you staying on in Cluj-Napoca, Herr Morrow, or, like me, traveling on to the Castle?" (There were several castles in Transylvania but there was only one that was ever spoken of.)

He smiled a predator's smile and for a moment I felt like prey. Then I pitied him if he thought I was. I knew how to deal with his kind.

"I am traveling to Castle Dracula, Doctor, to pay my respects to King Vlad and to thank him for the sanctuary he grants to me and those like me."

When Dracula took advantage of the chaos that followed both the Great War and the First Martian Invasion to form the Kingdom of Transylvania, his first royal decree was to grant asylum to those the world at large considered "monsters." There was no doubt that there were other asylum seekers who boarded first and would depart last so that no one could see their forms and faces or discern their natures. Most, however, would not travel to his castle but rather to the territories set aside for them.

Lunch was served in the dining room, a level above the main lounge. It had a less impressive view than the lounge, but we had gathered for cuisine, not the scenery.

Our meal was almost complete when Herr Rosin, who was sharing the table with the arms dealers and who seemed very friendly with them, exclaimed,

"*Mein Gott*, are we flying over Germany?"

"Is something the matter, Herr Rosin?" asked Lloyd, one of the arms dealers.

"*Der Führer* has restricted the Reich's airspace. Any craft passing over the Fatherland is to be shot down. Steward," Rosin shouted, "it may not be too late. Advise the Captain to turn about."

The steward, who like most of the crew was Romani, smiled and in accented German replied, "Not to worry, Major. All will be well with us."

Running to the window, Rosin looked down. "How can that be? We are passing over a Luftwaffe airfield as we speak."

As if on cue, two Messerschmitt BF 109s had taken off and were flying our way. This caused panic among most of the dinners. The nuns began praying. The newlyweds held each other close. Across the table from me. Frederick Morrow remained calm but seemed to get hairier. Only Sir Nigel and I remained seated, the others had apparently forgotten the nature of the *Carpathia*.

The Messerschmitts opened fire, bullets from their machines striking the fuselage and windows. But the *Carpathia* was constructed from reclaimed Martian metal, and the windows from super strong acrylic glass. It soon became apparent that the steward had been right–all would be well with *us*.

Not so the German planes. As had the pilots of the airplane

who had attacked Denham's Eighth Wonder of the World, the brave Luftwaffe airmen flew to attack us again. They were met with beams of solid light and then were no more. As debris from the planes fell to the ground, the beams struck again, this time raking the airfield from which the Messerschmitts had come. Noiseless explosions occurred on the ground, the sound having no more success than the German bullets in penetrating the body of the airship.

There was silence as well in the dining room as we realized the full import of what had just occurred. Transylvania had acquired more of the Martian technology than anyone had suspected.

The dining room began to empty. Morrow was the first to leave, explaining, "I should help calm the others." Soon there was only the staff, Sir Nigel, me, and a stunned Major Rosin. Slowly I approached the latter.

"Major, my condolences on the deaths of your countrymen. They fought bravely and died as warriors. May they be welcomed in Valhalla."

There were tears in his eyes as he rose from the table to acknowledge my comments.

"Thank you, Doctor. I am afraid that they will not be the last sacrifices to Mars. If you will excuse me, Fräulein, Sir Nigel."

We watched him leave, then Sir Nigel said, "Lesson learned."

Indeed, I thought, and the lesson was, "We will go where we want, when we want, and you cannot stop us." Wondering if the *Carpathia's* incursion into German airspace had been a deliberate incursion for the purpose of teaching this lesson, to both the German and British ambassadors, I returned to my cabin.

There were no further incidents. I spent the remainder of the flight composing a coded message to Holmes, informing him of the arms dealers' friendliness towards Rosin and the weaponry displayed by the *Carpathia*. Soon after I finished, we began our descent to the Cluj-Napoca aerodrome. I would ask Sir Nigel to send my message out by diplomatic courier before we left for Castle Dracula.

16

From the journal of Sherlock Holmes

Not since the affair of the Lion's Mane have I attempted to recount one of my own cases. The times I have done so makes me appreciate Watson's efforts on my behalf more than ever. It is one of my great regrets in life that I did not better express this appreciation to him when he was still alive.

At first, the theft of the Ring of Gyges seemed a simple affair. Wiggins, a former member of my Baker Street Irregulars and now an Inspector with Scotland Yard, had charge of the case.

"This Gyges ring, Mr. Holmes, was a gold ring on which a reddish ruby had been mounted. Engraved on the inside was writing in an unknown language."

I knew this, of course, having handled the ring several times when in the presence of its former owner, who has asked that neither Jane nor myself mention his name. But I allowed Wiggins to go on.

"It was donated to the museum by some professor of English and displayed right over there."

Wiggins pointed to an empty display stand on which the glass case in which the ring had been displayed had been.

"And what is your theory of the crime, Wiggins?"

Wiggins shrugged. "One of opportunity, Mr. Holmes. Our thief suddenly found himself alone in this room. He broke the glass, grabbed the ring, and left before anyone could discover the theft."

I looked around at the other exhibits–jewelry and precious gems from the age of antiquity, all of which outshone the ring in value and splendor. In fact, had it not been for the donor's professional stature and the fact that the ring was mentioned by Plato in his *Republic*, it would not have been displayed at all but regulated to storage.

After silently thanking the Lord that Jane's youthful infatuation with Wiggins had been short-lived, I decided not to mention any of this to him. Instead, I asked,

"What became of the broken glass, Wiggins. You inspected it, of course?"

Here he reddened, then stammered out, "Th … there was no need, Mr. Holmes, not for a simple smash and grab."

"Oh, Wiggins," I sighed. As proud as I am of Jane that is how disappointed I was at that time in Wiggins. "As I recall, you were with Watson and me in Baker Street when we were investigating the Affair of the Falcon of Malta. But for the fumbling of Lestrade, it would have been recovered and no doubt on exhibit in this very museum. Do you remember what it was I said when I learned of Lestrade's blunder, that there were no simple cases …"

At least Wiggins had the decency to look abashed as he completed the sentence, "Only simple policemen." I could tell by his face that he finally realized that my presence at the museum indicated that this was probably more than a simple "smash and grab."

"What's to be done, Mr. Holmes?"

"As I asked you before, what became of the broken glass?"

"I don't know, sir. We could find out."

"*You* could find out, Wiggins. I'll remain here to admire these ancient treasures."

Wiggins returned thirty minutes later, carrying a dusty paper sack. Behind him was an attendant who led us to a workroom where stood the remains of the display case.

"The glass had been swept up and placed in the bin. Fortunately, the dustmen have not yet been come. The case was to be repaired but they had not yet gotten to it."

Nodding my approval, I examined the case with my magnifying glass, finding a few fibers and a minute drop of what appeared to be blood. The thief had marked himself, or herself. (Ever since my first encounter with The Woman, I never fail to consider the fairer sex when it comes to crime.) I then examined the contents of the bag, finding one or two more fibers and several drops of suspected blood.

"Wiggins, take charge of the case and the broken glass. Have them examined for fingerprints."

"Any suspects, Mr. Holmes?"

As Jane and I had discussed, there was one, but I could not

discuss him with Wiggins. I shook my head, "Let us hope one will appear, Wiggins," I said, indulging myself with a bad pun. "Do let me know the results. Oh, and Wiggins?"

"Yes, Mr. Holmes."

"Jane tells me that you were a great help in apprehending Fantômas. He is still in custody, is he not?"

"Yes, Mr. Holmes. The last I checked, he was being held in the most secure cell in Strangeways."

"Let us hope, so, Wiggins, let us hope so."

17

On my return to Baker Street and after an excellent lunch, I conducted an analysis of the fibers I had recovered from the display case and broken glass. They were, as I had expected, physically identical in every way, which strongly indicated that they came from the same piece of clothing. I had once written a monograph on the regional identification of clothing through a study of its fibers. Sadly, thanks to the industrialization of the garment industry, it is now outdated and possibly obsolete. Still, in this case, I was able to determine that the garment, or at least the cotton from which the garment was made originated in or near Manchester. This, in itself, was not unusual in that Manchester was the center of England's textile trade.

However, as both my late friend and his daughter could relate, I dislike coincidences, and the fact that Strangeways Prison is also located in Manchester prompted me to call Wiggins.

"Yes, Mr. Holmes, what is it?"

"Have your forensic dactyloscopists finished with the evidence from the British Museum? If so, what have they found?"

"My what? Oh, the fingerprint men. Yes, they have, Mr. Holmes, and they recovered several identifiable lifts from the glass."

"Excellent. Convey to them my compliments and have them compare these prints against them."

When I gave Wiggins the name he said,

"That's impossible."

"Wiggins, since the Martians, nothing is impossible. Please, humor me in this. And you should call the warden of Strangeways, just in case. It may be that there is something important he has failed to report."

Wiggins called back within the hour. The prints, as I and most probably you who are reading this had expected, were identified as belonging to the master criminal Fantômas. It was not long after that that Wiggins and I were en route to Strangeways via a special train.

"I suppose Doctor Jane will be disappointed, Mr. Holmes. Given that she was the one who caught him."

"For two reasons, Wiggins. Shortly after his capture, I wagered her that Fantômas would escape before the end of this year. She thought it unlikely. As it is, she now owes me five pounds."

"Why did you think that he would escape?"

"It was back when you were running the Irregulars, Wiggins. It was a case I instructed Doctor Watson not to write up. Due to a … misunderstanding between myself and an Inspector Mackenzie, I found myself a … guest of Strangeways. Now while Mackenzie was a good man at catching cracksmen, excepting one that is, he was not the kind of man one would have investigate a murder. Thinking I was involved as more than an investigator, he arrested me and had me incarcerated. It took me only three days to escape and another two to solve the murder. When I turned the killer over to Lestrade, I made sure Mackenzie was present. Mackenzie's career stalled after that and he was transferred to Midsomer County."

"There is one thing I don't understand, Mr. Holmes."

"Just one, Wiggins?"

He ignored my jab and went on. "If Fantômas is such a clever crook, why didn't he wear gloves when he stole the ring?"

Again, Wiggins made me sigh. "Wiggins, you are a detective for whom, despite recent events such as the theft of the ring and the Harrison murder, I have great hopes. Stop and think about the man, his nature, and his character. He had been bested, by a woman no less. It was not enough for him merely to escape …"

Wiggins thought, then reasoned it out. "He left his prints deliberately. He was well, forgive me, Mr. Holmes, giving us the V and getting a bit of his own back."

"Very good, Wiggins, there may be hope for you yet."

"Thank you, Mr. Holmes. But why the Ring of Gyges? You've explained its significance to Doctor Jane, but Fantômas wasn't likely to know that?"

"A good question, Wiggins, one I hope to answer once we arrive at Strangeways."

When we arrived at the prison, Wiggins, in his capacity as a Scotland Yard Inspector, berated Warden Jones, demanding to know just how Fantômas escaped and why the Yard had not been informed.

"His Majesty's Prison Service was informed per procedure." the warden said defensively. "I can only suppose that they decided that it was not a matter for Scotland Yard. As to the manner of his escape, that is still under investigation."

"Then you are fortunate in that Sherlock Holmes is here to lend you his assistance."

At this, Warden Jones looked first at Wiggins, then at me. and then again at Wiggins. He did not seem to be impressed by either of us.

Ignoring me, Jones said to Wiggins, "I thank you for your offer, Inspector, but we are more than equipped to investigate on our own. We have no need of the services of an amateur, however talented some may believe him to be."

Amateur indeed. I get paid very well for what I do, except when I work *publico bono*. Except for exchanging greetings with the warden when we first entered, I spoke for the first time.

"Warden Jones, are you telling me that having allowed the third most dangerous person in all of Britain to escape, you are now refusing my help?" Before he could answer, I stood. Going over to his desk, I picked up the phone and dialed a number. Jones attempted to stop me, but a push from Wiggins sent him back into his chair.

"This is Holmes," I said. "Let me speak to M."

Once I was connected to Mycroft, I explained the situation. "Put the fool on," was all my brother said.

I handed the receiver to Jones and listened, admittedly with some delight, to the stammering coming from the warden. When Mycroft's tirade was over, Jones looked to me and said, "I have been instructed to give you my fullest cooperation, Mr. Holmes." It obviously pained him to say this and it pained him even more to add, "And may I offer my most humble apologies for the way I acted toward you both."

Wiggins and I both nodded our heads. Perhaps he took those

gestures as our acceptance of his apology, perhaps he did not. Neither of us cared.

"Please show us to Fantômas's cell," I said. "Forgive me, former cell. I trust it has remained unoccupied."

"Yes, Mr. Holmes, it has. I'll have someone escort you there."

Wiggins then spoke up. "Forgive me, Warden, but Mr. Holmes asked that *you* show us to the cell. We can speak along the way."

As the three of us walked to the cell, Warden Jones summarized the guards' report of the incident.

"The prisoner was alone in the cell block to which there was only one exit. It was at night, with two guards, Newman and Fitzroy, on duty, both outside a locked gate. The clock had just struck a quarter past one when Fitzroy fell as if struck from behind."

"What, if anything, did Newman see or do when this happened?" Wiggins asked.

"He reported that, suspecting a sudden illness, he rushed to the fellow's aid. When he bent over him, he too was struck down."

"Did he see his assailant?"

"No, Inspector, he claimed that all he saw was a baton coming through the air toward him."

"And did he see the man who was holding the baton?"

"That's just it, Inspector, Newman says that there was no one holding the baton. That it came down on him all on its own. That is why we have not been able to conclude our investigations as we are not sure that there was no collusion between the guards and the prisoner."

I could have offered an explanation, but neither Wiggins nor Jones would have believed me.

We came to the cell block in which Fantômas had been housed. Warden Jones and I spent the next hour watching Wiggins as he thoroughly examined the cell for a means of escape. He sounded the floor and tried the bars. Thus was, of course, no keyhole on the inside of the door and so he tried to reach the hole on the outside. Despite having a longer reach than Fantômas, he could not do so. Finally, he gave up.

"I'm beat, Mr. Holmes. I suppose now you'll show me what I

missed. Maybe have yourself locked in then miraculously open the door like that Houdini fellow might have."

It was thanks to the tricks shown to me by my late friend Houdini that I was able to escape my cell in Strangeways, but there was no need to mention that. But none of those tricks would have worked for this cell.

"Not this time, Inspector. You did as well as I did."

"Then that means …"

"Yes, Wiggins, that Fantômas had help in escaping."

"The guards, I knew it," exclaimed the warden.

"Perhaps," I allowed. "Are they still in the infirmary?"

"Yes, they were both struck very hard, or at least one was. The other no doubt injured himself, but which one?"

"Please take us to them, Warden."

The guards' section of the infirmary had been isolated from the rest by means of a screen. The two were, ironically, under guard themselves. At my insistence, I spoke to them alone, even to the point of temporarily dismissing their guard.

"I am Sherlock Holmes. If you answer my questions truthfully I can help you. Otherwise, you are both likely to be dismissed with the stain of suspicion on you."

They looked at each other, then the one called Fitzroy answered. "Ask us what you will, Mr. Holmes."

Under my questioning, they related the same story they had told the warden. When they were finished, I asked, "Did you both fully lose consciousness?"

"I did," Newman said. "Right after that baton was thrown at me."

"Someone threw it, then?"

"They must have, Mr. Holmes. How else?"

"How else indeed, Newman. Fitzroy, what about you?"

"I blacked out for a moment, Mr. Holmes. I came to just as Newman went down, or I thought I did. Maybe I didn't. Because what I thought I saw was so impossible that I didn't mention it to anyone."

I bent low to Fitzroy and in a whisper meant only for his ears said, "Floating keys."

His eyes widened in surprise as he asked, "How did you know, sir?"

"Because," I said, "I am Sherlock Holmes."

With my interview over and my suspicions confirmed, I went to where Wiggins and Jones were standing, To the warden I said,

"Newman and Fitzroy are innocent. Once they are fit, please return them to duty without a stain on their records."

"But why, Mr. Holmes?"

"I cannot answer that, Warden Jones."

"But I need a reason."

"Then do it because, as a representative of His Majesty's government, I order you to."

"Very well, Mr. Holmes," the warden said reluctantly.

18

On the train back to London, before Wiggins could ask, I said, "Forgive me if I do not explain myself as I usually do, Wiggins, but this is a matter of the utmost secrecy."

"I understand Mr. Holmes, but would you permit me to apply your methods."

How could I have refused? So we sat in silence as Wiggins, his eyes closed and his brow furrowed, went over all he knew and had seen about the case. Finally, his eyes opened and he asked, "Have you ever read any of the works of H. G. Wells, Mr. Holmes?" After I allowed that I had, Wiggins said, "I am particularly fond of the novel featuring a man named Griffin. What about you, sir?"

I was amazed and had to ask myself if this was the same detective who had failed to properly investigate the theft of the Ring of Gyges.

"How did you come to this conclusion?"

He quoted my own words to me. "Once you eliminate the impossible, whatever remains, no matter how improbable, must be the truth. But the problem is, Mr. Holmes, that you yourself said that these days nothing is impossible so this was the only possible conclusion."

"Very good, Wiggins," I said, "You do yourself proud. Jane would be impressed."

"Thank you, sir. And I do understand that I am not to mention this to anyone, not that they would believe me. But there is one thing I would like to ask."

"And that is?"

"The third most dangerous person in Britain? Who then are the other two?"

"The name of the most dangerous person I cannot reveal. Their identity is above your level. As for the second, well, modesty forbids me from saying."

We spent the rest of the trip recollecting old cases in which the Baker Street Irregulars were involved. After we parted, I returned to Baker Street and prepared a coded message to Jane. As it would not reach her until her arrival at Dracula's Castle, I prayed it would not arrive too late.

19

From the diary of Jane Watson
As the *Carpathia* approached the Cluj-Napoca Aerodrome it took time to circle the field. It was there that we saw the full extent of Dracula's embrace of Martian weaponry. Tripods patrolled the perimeter of the field, their death rays shining and at the ready. Despite my knowledge of their presence, the sight of them sent a chill through my body as I remembered the devastation they had caused during the Second Invasion. I'm sure the other passengers felt the same, and several moved away from the windows so as not to see them. Another warning from the King of Transylvania of the folly of invading his country. Another reason for me to make sure that if he was not for the British he was, at least, not against us.

As the airship was landing, the passengers were advised that due to the lateness of the hour, those of us who were traveling on to Castle Dracula would be accommodated at the aerodrome hotel for the night. Those traveling to the "special reserve" would be transported there immediately.

The customs search was extremely thorough. No weapons were allowed, nor any objects made of silver. This included coins, medallions, religious items, and the like. The first to object to this were the Anglican nuns, whose silver crosses and chains were taken from them with the promise of the item's return if they left the country. However, they were offered plain wooden crosses in place of the ones confiscated. They accepted them and reluctantly slipped the leather thongs over their necks.

The newlyweds were concerned about their rings (mixed gold and silver), but as they were remaining in Cluj-Napoca they were allowed to keep them.

Frederick Morrow merely laughed when asked if he had silver on his person or luggage, which only confirmed my suspicions about him. He then showed the customs officer a document. This caused them to take one or two steps back and allow him to proceed without any further inspection.

Both Herr Rosin and Sir Nigel complained the loudest, stating that as ambassadors to the court of His Majesty they were exempt from having their luggage and their persons searched. As Herr Rosin was demanding, in his best Teutonic hauteur, to speak with the customs officers' supervisor, I again reminded Sir Nigel of the Turkish Ambassadors, their hats, and Vlad Tepes's macabre sense of the ironic. In turn, he had a quiet word with Rosin and the two submitted to a search. I later learned that the search was quite thorough and involved examination gloves.

I had little trouble with customs, allowing Officers Verger and Bodrogi to search my luggage. Being well aware of what items were and were not permitted, I made sure that none were in any of my bags. In addition, knowing that custom officials are much the same anywhere in the world, I had placed a small bottle of Jamison's best whiskey as well as several delicacies unavailable in Transylvania on top of my belongings. These, of course, were confiscated "just in case," which assured the safe and proper handling of the rest of my possessions.

As for my person, I was not about to have strangers place their hands on me. Instead, like Frederick Morrow, I showed them a document, one that identified me as a "special and honored guest of His Majesty King Vlad, one who was to be afforded all courtesies."

This presented the custom officials with a problem, one I quickly solved. "Of course, I can always depart on the *Carpathia* when it returns to England, sending word to His Majesty as to why I was not able to attend him as he commanded."

They passed me through without a physical search after having me swear that I carried nothing silver. I did so swear, for indeed I did not. I did not need to smuggle in silver weapons to kill a vampire. I had other means at my disposal, or so I hoped.

"You understand, Doctor, that you are ... staking your life on your oath," Verger said.

Smiling in appreciation of the pun and the warning, I replied. "I do, and I thank you both. Be assured I will inform His Majesty of your courtesy, efficiency, and professionalism."

20

That night at dinner I sat with the two arms dealers and played the ingénue, learning much about their business dealings with Germany, the Soviets, as well as their hopes to license King Vlad's Martian technology. Peter Lloyd seemed enthused about this prospect. His partner, Christopher Falk, seemed less excited, possibly because he already knew the futility of asking Vlad to share his wonderful toys.

To my surprise, Sir Henry and Herr Rosin shared a table, perhaps having one last convivial meal before their countries' actions made them enemies. Frederick Morrow ate his meal with the nuns. Whatever stories he was telling them made the two younger ones laugh. The older nun, one Sister Regis, did not appear to be amused.

After dinner, most of the company traveling to the castle remained to enjoy music and conversation. Having additional secret messages for the diplomatic pouch that was to go out on the *Carpathia* in the morning, I elected to turn in early and said my goodnights.

I was almost at the stairs when,

"Doctor Watson."

"Yes, Herr Morrow?"

"Please, call me Frederick. I was wondering if later tonight you might be interested in having a nightcap, either in my room or in yours."

I did not need Holmes's elixir to detect the pheromones coming from Morrow. Their musky yet subtle aroma invoked in me passion, sensuality, and lust. While I'm sure that Morrow had had great success with a great many women, I was made of sterner stuff and had prepared myself for such a sensory onslaught.

"Thank you, but no, Herr Morrow," I said.

"Perhaps another night?"

Even as he asked this, I saw Morrow glance toward Sister Regis and her two charges, Sisters Miriam and Teresa. In a harsh whisper,

I said,

"Herr Morrow, I am no man's *cane*, nor do I practice *coitus more ferarum*. (The latter, I must confess, was a lie.) And if I find out that you have been sniffing around the nuns for more than moral and spiritual guidance, well, please know that I have been trained in certain veterinary techniques. Good night, Herr Morrow. "

With that, I returned to my room, finished my work, and slept the sleep of the morally just, albeit with an interesting dream or two, the contents of which are no one's business save mine.

21

The following morning, those of us traveling to Castle Dracula were gathered in the hotel's dining room for breakfast. In addition to the passengers of the *Carpathia*, there were several men and women who sat separate from the rest of us. There was a bureaucratic look about them. I surmised that they were in service to the state or to the king himself and were returning to the castle to report on whatever mission had drawn them away.

I observed these people deferring to a woman and had heard the hotel manager refer to her as "Lady Alina." Sir Nigel was sitting next to me and on seeing my interest in this woman, said quietly, "Alina Renfield. She is King Vlad's majordomo and all but runs the castle for him."

On hearing "Renfield" all became clear. The original Renfield was a madman at Doctor John Seward's asylum who was seduced by Dracula, who turned him into his thrall. It is now less a name than a title for anyone in personal service to King Vlad, who ensures their loyalty with a blood exchange. Unless one has a very strong will, once this exchange takes place, the only means of escape from this bondage is release by Dracula or death. Still, it is believed that the renfields enter into this servitude willingly, as it is the only way for one to advance in government service. Rare is the manager who is not a renfield.

Alina Renfield was a small, dark-haired woman who appeared to be in her late teens. However, she carried herself as one who was much older. Although she looked nothing like her, she reminded me of Katherine Barnaby, who, I had to keep reminding myself, was really Professor Moriarty in a stolen body.

Curious, I approached Lady Alina on the pretext of getting more tea. As I passed her, I felt the same small *frisson* of excitement as I did when I was near Moriarty. It was not sexual attraction–despite an experience in Paris I was not carnally inclined towards women–but something else, something I heretofore had only felt with my parents and Uncle Sherlock, that of belonging.

Nonsense, I told myself. But if that were so, why did I feel Lady Alina's eyes on me, and why, when I sat back down at my table, did I observe her watching me?

When breakfast was over, the hotel manager addressed us, expressing his wishes that we had enjoyed our stay and wishing us success in our endeavors. He then introduced Lady Alina who addressed our group.

"On behalf of His Majesty King Vlad, I bid you welcome to his kingdom of Transylvania. For security reasons, no aircraft are permitted in the area around His Majesty's castle. Ground transportation will be provided. We will depart after lunch and break our journey at the Borgo Inn. We will remain there for most of the day before continuing to His Majesty's castle where he will greet you, his honored guests, at dinner. May I suggest that you use this time to acclimate yourself to the nocturnal schedule that His Majesty and his court follow."

As I was about to leave, Lady Alina stopped me. "Doctor Watson?"

"Yes, Lady Alina?"

"I must tell you, Doctor, that 'Lady' is a courtesy title. To be honest, it is more than I deserve."

"I am sure, Lady Alina, that because of the service you render for King Vlad you deserve that and more."

"Thank you, Doctor. The reason I stopped you, and please forgive me, but have we met before?"

So she had felt it too, that feeling of recognition. From the way she asked, I suspected that she might know more about it than I.

"No, I would have remembered."

"That's right, you work for Sherlock Holmes. You remember everything."

"I work *with* Sherlock Holmes," I not so gently reminded her, "and yes, I try to remember all that is important to my cases. Speaking of which, is there anything you can tell about the reason His Majesty had requested me?"

"King Vlad has made it clear to me that he wishes to brief you on that matter personally." Taking my hand, Lady Alina gently squeezed it. "Perhaps we can speak later, on the bus, or at the hotel."

With that she departed, leaving me to wonder of what she wanted to speak. Perhaps it was merely a gesture of friendship. She may not know many women with whom she can speak on a personal level. Or perhaps she wanted more than friendship. Either way, an ally close to King Vlad would be useful. If need be, I would do what I had to do, for King and Country.

Before I could go up to my room, I heard "Doctor Watson." Turning, I saw Frederick Morrow standing by the stairs. I considered giving him the cut direct but settled for an icy "Herr Morrow."

"Doctor Watson, may we speak privately?"

I allowed that we could and we went outside. "Doctor Watson, I beg of you to forgive my actions of last night. My conduct was reprehensible. From your words to me I am sure that you are aware of my condition. My only excuse for my behavior is that sometimes my curse overwhelms me and my bestial side takes over."

True or not, it was a proper apology. He would bear watching but as we were traveling together …

"There are no bodies for the Cluj-Napoca police to find?"

Morrow shook his head. "None that I left."

"And you did not awake this morning naked and bloody?"

He smiled. "Not bloody. As for the other, I do not like pajamas."

"Then you are forgiven, Herr Morrow. But keep your bestial side under control, or the closest you will come to King Vlad is a stake outside his castle."

22

That there was a limit to how much technology King Vlad had obtained from the Martians was proved by the "ground transportation" provided. Waiting for us was a Benz omnibus that appeared to be at least a decade old. However, it was well maintained and I was sure that it was more than capable of delivering us to our destination.

Like the other passengers, I had kept with me a small case containing what was needed for an overnight stay. In addition, I had also kept my medical bag with me, not wanting to chance its contents falling into the wrong hands.

The roads of Transylvania are not the streets of London. The trip was rough and at times bumpy. I found myself looking forward to the hotel, however rustic it may be. As Lady Alina spent most of the journey talking with Sir Nigel and Herr Rosin, I occupied my time observing her.

The evening before I had noticed that the renfields all shared a certain demeanor, as if their service to Dracula was ever foremost in their mind. I wondered if it were possible for King Vlad to monitor or even control them from afar, and if so, what the range of this power was. I made a mental note to discuss this with Mycroft and Holmes on my return.

Lady Alina, however, did not share this demeanor. In comparison to the others, she seemed remarkably alert and self-possessed, rather than being possessed by another, however minimally.

From the brief conversation we had the evening before I judged from her unique accent that she had originally been Swiss. Holmes would probably have known from what canton but I am not he.

The first hints of evening had arrived by the time we reached our destination. The Borgo Inn was not what I expected. It was a large structure, well-suited to accommodate those journeying to and from Castle Dracula. It had a pub which catered to both travelers and locals alike.

After a washup and a rest, I went down to the pub for dinner. Although we were seated apart from the locals, their voices were clear to us, even if I could not understand them.

I was sharing a table with Lady Alina. "Why does His Majesty permit nuns, My Lady?" I asked. "I would have thought he'd be opposed to all things religious?"

"The king," she replied, "is not a superstitious man. The rumor of not caring for crosses or holy water is unfounded. He believes in no higher power than himself. But he realizes that some need the consolation of religion. He will not have priests, so he has allowed the nuns to come to attend the spiritual needs of his guests."

Just then Frederick Morrow came over and politely asked if he could join us. She had no objections and so I allowed him to do so. Midway through our meal, Morrow, noting as I had that the voices coming from the area around the bar were loud and getting louder, said,

"They seem to be arguing about something."

"More upset and scared, I would think," I offered. Although I did not speak the language–which seemed to be a mixture of Romanian, Hungarian, and Romani–I recognized fear when I heard it. *What*, I wondered, *could frighten people whose king was a vampire?* "Alina, could you enlighten us?"

She hesitated, as if not wanting to expose the fears of Vlad's subjects to outsiders. But then she listened, translating as she did so.

"Do either of you know the meaning of the word *vârcolac*?"

"Werewolf," answered Morrow.

"Yes, Herr Morrow, I thought you might." Lady Alina looked around. If the renfields understood what the locals were saying, they had decided that it was not their concern. Falk and Lloyd were dining with Herr Rosin, while Sir Nigel was eating alone. From time to time, he would look over at the empty chair next to him. There was a worried look on his face as if he were nervous about his assignment as ambassador to the Court of Vlad Tepes.

After assuring herself that she would not be overheard, Lady Alina said, "Over the past fortnight, there have been several attacks on cattle in the area. They look to be the work of a large beast. Last night, a woman was killed in a similar manner. People are scared and nervous. This evening the two men at the end of the bar, outsiders named Mihai Dalca and Darius Bogdan, said that they had been hunting a *vârcolac* and that it sounded like this was the work of that beast. They have offered to kill it."

"For how much?" I asked.

Lady Alina shook her head. "Dalca and Bogdan have volunteered their services but have said that they needed silver to melt down to make the bullets that can kill the beast."

"I thought silver was forbidden?"

"At the castle, Herr Morrow, and in the protected areas, but not in general."

Morrow stood up. "You ladies will please excuse me."

"Herr Morrow," I warned, "Do not do anything foolish."

"Do not worry, Doctor, I did that once a long time ago in Cologne and have been paying the price ever since. I merely wish to take a…look around."

"Then I shall go with you. Lady Alina, would you please stay here and continue to listen?"

"Very well, Doctor. But do not take long." She indicated the crowd, which seemed to be getting more and more excited.

Outside, I followed Morrow as he walked around the inn, his bestial nature coming to the fore as he sniffed the air. Not knowing what was going to occur, I was grateful for the dagger I had slid up my right sleeve before coming down to dinner. Its blade was, of course, not silver, but a thrust into an ear, eye, or heart would kill any creature of this world.

We made two circuits of the grounds. After we had finished, Morrow, once again more man than beast, said, "Nothing. None of my kind are anywhere close."

"That makes Dalca and Bogdan…"

Morrow interrupted me. "Confidence men and tricksters."

"I was going to say murder suspects. Remember the woman killed two nights ago. But we'd best make sure."

We went back inside. Dalca and Bogdan had departed. Sitting back down, Morrow looked at Lady Alina and shook his head.

"The locals have agreed to bring the silver tomorrow night."

"Then you'd best send a messenger to the king and tell him that we're going to be delayed."

Alina glared at me. "One does not tell a king, especially King Vlad, anything, Doctor. We are expected tomorrow night."

"Then when you arrive at his castle, please advise the king that Doctor Watson has been delayed on a matter of justice, His Majesty's Justice, and that she will attend him when she has completed what you dared not do."

Another glare, this time I returned it. So much for our friendship. After a few tense moments, Lady Alina stood and walked over to one of the renfields. There was a muted discussion during which the renfield grew increasingly paler. Finally, he nodded and Lady Alina returned.

"A message will be sent. This close to the castle it will be easy. The others will continue and arrive tomorrow evening. The omnibus will then return for the three of us. Now then, Doctor, what do you plan to do?"

I told her. She went over and spoke with the innkeeper. She must have mentioned Dracula's name because he straightened up as if at attention. After he nodded several times, Lady Alina returned to our table.

"The body is at the church, being prepared for burial. You may examine it tomorrow morning. You had best be right." She looked at me then at Morrow. "Both of you."

I would have liked to have said something like, "I am the goddaughter of Sherlock Holmes and I am always right," but I preferred to do my bragging after the case is solved and not before. So instead, I said my goodnights to Lady Alina and Frederick Morrow and went to bed.

An hour later I was awakened by laughter and voices coming from the room next to mine. Morrow's room.

"Don't worry," I heard him say, "I promise not to bite."

Given the circumstances, I didn't think him fool enough to have seduced one of the local women, and dallying with one of the two females renfields was just too dangerous. That only left…

"Wouldn't matter if you did, Frederick."

Lady Alina.

Silently I wished them joy. Then I wished that they would not take too long or be too loud in achieving it.

They quieted after about thirty minutes. I spent my time considering the problem of Alina Renfield. She was King Vlad's majordomo yet she was not able to communicate with him over a distance as could other renfields. And she was not concerned about a werewolf bite. Rather, from what I heard, I think she enjoyed it. There was that *frisson* I had felt when we first met, the same I felt with Moriarty and with Holmes when we used his elixir. Coupled with her Swiss accent, this led me to the only conclusion. Satisfied in a way other than the two in the next room were, I closed my eyes and slept soundly.

23

The next morning, Lady Alina, Morrow, and I went to the Church of Saint Sabbas to view the body. The priest who met us was old, well past the age at which he should have retired, and visibly nervous about receiving a representative of Vlad's Court.

Although not openly hostile to religion, the king did not hide his disdain for it. Understandable, given that the Christian, Jewish, and Moslem faiths all formally condemned him as an instrument of Satan. However, his opposition to organized religion had caused open belief in his country to wither away. There were few converts among the young, and no ministers to replace those that passed away or gave up.

Father Paul's "Welcome" was less than enthusiastic.

Lady Alina did not help the situation by saying, "Paul Balan, we are here on the authority of His Majesty King Vlad."

Father Paul's face lost all color and I could tell that he thought we had come for him, to shut down his church and possibly drag him to martyrdom at Castle Dracula. I wondered if she had done this deliberately and if so why. Did she share her master's views on religion and its representatives?

To relieve the priest's mind, I said in Latin,

"Father, I am Doctor Jane Watson. I was traveling to the castle of His Majesty when I heard of the tragedy that befell Maria Ciobanu. My companions and I are here to examine her body. We wish to determine who has done this terrible thing and see that God's Justice is done."

Father Paul's face brightened as color returned to it. *"What of her?"* he asked, looking at Lady Alina.

I had learned Latin at the University. I needed it for my medical studies and the research Holmes had me do. Unsure if either of my companions understood it, I took Father Paul aside. *"They will accompany me, the woman as the king's witness and the man as my secretary."*

The priest cast an experienced eye over both. *"He is more than a man, and less of one, is he not?"*

"Yes, he is, but he is not the one we seek. I will vouch for his behavior."

"See that you do, Doctor, or I will account for him and her if I can."

As I have said, Father Paul was old, but with his years came experience. Now that he knew that we had not come for him, he seemed ready to confront that which he believed to be evil.

"Please show us the body," I said, then repeated my words in English.

There was an alcove off the altar to the priest's left. In it was a table on which was the cloth-covered body of Maria Ciobanu. Father Paul led us to it.

"You will be respectful, will you not?"

"Father, what better way to respect the dead than to obtain justice for them? Now then, what can you tell me about her?"

According to Father Paul, Maria was the only child of Ionut and Elana Ciobanu. By all accounts, she was a "good girl" in every respect. She did not yet have a steady beau but was mostly interested in a young man named Andre Eder and friendly with Gheorghei Hofer and Marcu Ioveanu. Her closest female friend was Sofia Muller. When I asked, he reluctantly told me where these people could be found.

From my bag, I took out a notebook and pen. Handing them to Morrow I said, "Take notes." To Lady Alina, "Please translate what I say for Father Paul." Seeing that she was about to object, I added, "It is his church. He has a right to know."

I attended my first autopsy at the age of twelve. It was my birthday present from Sherlock Holmes. From the minute the doctor's knife opened the body to reveal its wonders I knew that I wanted to be a physician like my father. As when Holmes deduced the identity of the killer solely from the results of the autopsy, I also knew that I wanted to be like him as well. And now these twin realizations had led me to a village church in the middle of Transylvania where I was about to examine the victim of a presumed werewolf.

Donning mask and gloves, I gently removed the sheet from the dead woman. She was still dressed in the tattered remains of a blouse and skirt. She must have been taken right from the murder scene to the church. That was good. It meant that any evidence on her clothing might still be there.

Using a torch and my glass, I began my examination, narrating my actions as I went along. "Subject's clothing is ripped and torn to the point of falling off her body. It would be useful although not necessary to have any remnants that were not recovered from the scene. The clothing is stained with dirt and blood. There are no indications that any of the bloodstains are not hers, but I will take representatives samples should they be needed."

I paused to allow Morrow to catch up then continued.

"The subject's nails were not well maintained but this appears to be their usual condition. There are no recent breaks or tears, nor are there any traces of flesh or blood beneath them."

Carefully and respectfully, I removed Maria's clothing. As I did so, I noticed Father Paul move back so that, while he could still observe the proceedings, he could not clearly see Maria's naked body.

Another toe to head examination with torch and glass. Her lower body did not bear any wounds, nor were there any signs of sexual molestation.

Her body from navel on up was savagely mutilated.

"Herr Morrow, please come close." When Morrow did I said, "Tell me what you see."

"What I see, Doctor, is a mess. She's been opened up but her organs are more or less intact. None of have been devoured as a beast would have."

"Thank you, Herr Morrow, it is always good to get the opinion of an … expert. Please, step back."

Using my scalpel, I cut away what flesh I had to in order to better examine her ribs. Some were fractures, others bore marks similar to that of an ax, a unique ax, one with a chipped blade.

After seeing this, I gave Morrow my final note, an observation that I had made at the start but which I held back for maximum effect.

"The subject's throat was cut from behind by a left-handed person standing approximately 1.7 meters tall."

After filling a vial with her blood, I covered Maria's body with the sheet and said, in English for Lady Alina and Morrow and Latin for Father Paul, "I, Doctor Jane Watson, acting in the name of His Majesty King Vlad, do solemnly swear and affirm that Maria Ciobanu met her death by human hands and not by any beast fair or foul, natural or unnatural." I then added, for Father Paul's sake and the sake of Maria's family, "Father, other than those left by the person who killed her, I found no traces of evil in the body of Maria Ciobanu. She may be buried in holy ground as she is."

The priest ran over to me. Taking both of my hands in his, he shook them. He also placed two things in them, one of which went up my left sleeve. The other I held up for all to see.

It was a silver crucifix. "Thank you, Father," I said, still alternating between English and Latin, "But it is more than I deserve or have earned. Besides, I travel to the King's Castle, where, as you know, such items are…discouraged."

Pleased with his successful deception, Father Paul smiled. "Then I will keep it for you, Doctor, for when you return on your journey home."

I left the Church of Saint Sabbas with a dagger up my left sleeve, a sister to the one up my right, only this one I was sure had a silver blade.

On the way back to the inn Morrow asked, "So, Doctor Watson, which one killed her? Dalca and Bogdan?"

"Why do you ask that?"

"In talking to the priest you said, 'the person who killed her,' and not 'the people who killed her.' That means only one of them killed her, doesn't it?"

"Yes. The blows were consistent with a single killer. It does not mean that either one of them is the killer."

"Why do you say that, Doctor?" Lady Alina asked.

"Either is of the right height but did either of you notice if Dalca or Bogdan were left-handed?" Both shook their heads. "Neither did I." (Holmes would have, and if he ever reads this he will be very disappointed in me.)

"Herr Morrow, you were close to Maria's body. Did you get her scent and do you retain it in your olfactory memory?"

Morrow did not take my question kindly. "Yes," he bristled. "Why?"

"I have a job suited to your talents."

He was even less pleased when I told him what it was. "In case you need a reminder," and handed him the bundle of Maria's clothing.

"It will take some time," he said.

I tore a page from my notebook. On it, I wrote the names Father Paul had given me and how they might be found. "Start with these."

"When do you need this done?" he asked.

"Take as much time as you need but be finished by this evening."

Morrow glared at me, his eyes turning red. He turned to Lady Alina as if in appeal.

"You seek the favor of King Vlad, Herr Morrow," she said in a harsh tone. "If you wish to earn it, I suggest you get started."

With a snarl that reminded me how near his bestial side was to the surface, he was off.

As we watched him leave, Lady Alina said, "I do hope he does not get caught. He was…entertaining." She then added, "You were right, Doctor, this did bear investigating. I believe His Majesty will be pleased."

So we were friends again, or at least friendly.

No further words passed between us until we reached the inn. On our return, I noticed that the bus which had taken the rest of our party to Castle Dracula had returned, bringing with it three very large Romani. There was also a carriage. The Romani bowed to us, or rather, to Lady Alina, but otherwise remained with the bus. I thought I knew why they had come. When I asked Lady Alina about them, she allowed that I was correct.

"There will be much to do tonight, both here and at the castle," Lady Alina said. "We should rest." When I agreed she asked, "Will you join me?"

King and country be damned. I had neither the desire nor the inclination. Besides, who knew what she may have picked up from Morrow. Declining her offer, I went alone to my room for a nap.

24

The evening it seemed as if the entire town and countryside had turned out to meet and deal with the fearless werewolf hunters. Many had brought silver with them–coins, jewelry, religious items, all to be sacrificed for the greater good of ridding their land of the *vârcolac*. Thinking he might be needed, I had sent a note to Saint Sabbas asking Father Paul to come. Seeing him at a far table, Lady Alina sat with him. With Father Paul's help, I was able to identify Maria's friends and so study them. One stood out.

Morrow had yet to arrive and I worried that he might have run into trouble or simply have run away. Either was preferable to having the wolf inside him take over. I thought of the silver dagger now strapped to my inner left thigh and hoped I would not have to use it.

Evening was fading into night when Dalca and Bogdan entered the pub. Thankfully, Morrow was right behind them. Catching my eye, he motioned for me to meet him outside.

When I went outside, Lady Alina's Romani were nowhere in sight. Presumably, they were still on the bus.

"You were right," Morrow said, taking a hand ax from beneath his coat and giving it to me. Yes, it had the chipped blade I had expected.

"Where did you find it?"

He told me, adding, "But you were inside the pub. You probably already knew that."

"I had a strong suspicion which this confirms. I only need one thing more."

"What do you want me to do?"

"Remain out here, Herr Morrow. Other than Dalca and Bogdan, stop anyone who tries to leave."

"And how am I supposed to do that?"

"Be charming. If that doesn't work, scare the *rahat* out of them."

"So you picked up some Romanian?"

"Only the worst kind. Thank you, Herr Morrow, you did well today."

He seemed so pleased at this compliment I had to resist the urge to pat his head and say, "Who's a good boy?"

By the time I went back inside Dalca and Bogdan had begun collecting silver. On seeing me, Lady Alina stood to play her part.

"*Your attention please,*" she said loud enough so that everyone paused. (I was relying on Father Paul to translate.) "*I am the Lady Alina Renfield and I am here as the representative of His Majesty King Vlad.*"

If it was quiet before, now there was dead silence. I looked at Dalca and Bogdan, wondering if they were about to flee. That might have been the smart thing to do, which is one of the reasons I had left Morrow outside on guard.

Dalca and Bogdan stood their ground, although they did turn slightly pale when she addressed them directly.

"*Mihai Dalca and Darius Bogdan, on behalf of His Majesty, I would like to thank you for helping to rid this land of evil such as the vârcolac.*" Then to assembled folk. "*King Vlad wishes you to know that because of his great love for his subjects, he does not want you to suffer any further loss. And while, for obvious reasons, His Majesty has no silver of his own...*" Lady Alina paused to allow for some respectful laughter, "*... He will reimburse all those who provide it to these fearless men. Innkeeper, pen and paper please.*"

The landlord rushed to provide the request objects which Lady Alina handed to Dalca and Bogdan.

"You will please make a list of all the silver you have so far collected and will collect so that His Majesty may compensate these good people."

This is when Dalca and Bogdan should have fled. Up until then, they had merely been cheating simple folk. Now, however, they were cheating the king. But instead of running for their lives, they began to make their lists. Both of them used their right hands, thus sealing someone else's doom.

The collection of the silver took another thirty minutes. When it was over, Dalca and Bogdan signed their inventories which Lady

Alina also signed on behalf of King Vlad.

Placing the jewelry, coins, and holy items in a purple bag, Lady Alina handed it to them. "You had best be gone now," she said, escorting the pair to the door.

Morrow later told me that no sooner were Dalca and Bogdan than the Romani swiftly took the two into custody and put them on the bus.

The first part of the evening was over. With Father Morrow translating my Latin, it was my turn to address the crowd.

"Good people," I said, *"I am Doctor Jane Watson of Great Britain, a country with much love for King Vlad and his people. It is my hope that our two countries will always be friends and allies."* There were some murmurs of agreement at this but mostly stares encouraging me to get on with my business.

"I, too, am here as a representative of King Vlad, charged with looking into the tragic death of Maria Ciobanu." Now they were interested. *"It is my sad duty to report to you that she was not killed by the werewolf but rather by someone she knew. Someone present in this room."*

I love this part of being a detective–gathering the suspects and revealing the killer, who hopefully will try to escape but won't.

The crowd was excited now. There were shouts of what I took to be disbelief, others from those demanding to know who the killer was, and others from those who wanted to know just who this interfering outsider was. (Father Paul later confirmed that all three of my suppositions were correct.)

I quieted the crowd by holding up the vial I had filled during Maria's autopsy. *"This is the blood of Maria Ciobanu. It is well known that the blood of a murder victim will boil when it gets close to her killer."*

Slowly I walked through the crowd, each of them shying away from me and the vial I held as if there was something unholy about it and me. I went past Sofia Muller and Gheorghei Hofer. I then approached the table where sat Andre Eder and Marcu Ioveanu.

The blood was warm in my hand. *"Andre Eder, will you take the vial into yours?"*

Reaching out with his right hand, he took it eagerly saying, *"I loved her. I did not, could not kill her."*

I then turned to Marcu who did not disappoint. Most killers are a superstitious and cowardly lot and he proved this by running from the table and pushing his way through the surprised crowd to the door. Once outside, there was a growl and a cry of horror.

As one, the whole of the inn ran outside to find a very human-looking Frederick Morrow standing over the prostrate form of Marcu Ioveanu. The young man had soiled himself and was shaking as if he had seen the only real werewolf in the area.

A man Father Paul identified as Maria's father came through the crowd and confronted the young man.

"Why?" he asked. *"Why did you do this?"*

Marcu looked up. Through his tears and panic, he managed to say, *"I wanted her but she wanted Andre. Now no one has her."*

"God does," Father Paul said quietly. But the crowd was in no mood for God or His Mercy.

Some of the crowd got Marcu to his feet. As they dragged him away the landlord, after talking to Maria's father, came up to Lady Alina and me.

"My ladies, I know you are here on the King's business and it is the right of the King to punish those who break his laws. But I am, we are, asking you, no, begging you to permit us, on behalf of His Majesty, to punish this one."

Lady Alina told me what the innkeeper had asked. "Your country, your laws, your decision," I said.

Turning to the innkeeper Lady Alina nodded. Then he and the rest of the crowd set off in search of a rope. There were plenty of trees.

The bus was gone along with the Romani and their two charges. Our carriage to Castle Dracula awaited. There was enough of the night for us to arrive by sunrise but my meeting with Dracula would have to wait for the following evening.

With what little luggage we had packed, we set out. Remembering Stoker's novel, I could not help but wonder if our driver was the King of Transylvania. As I was chiding myself for such fancies, Morrow asked,

"What going to happen with the silver?" Before they left, the Romani had given the bag to Lady Alina.

She shrugged. "It will be returned to the village."

"If I may, Lady Alina?"

"Yes, Doctor?"

"The village has just suffered two deaths. One the murder of a young woman. The other the execution of her killer. The first will leave a scar. The other, however justified, will leave a stain. For you to return the silver, for them to learn how they were fooled might destroy them."

"What do you suggest?"

"Sell the silver, send the money to the village. Ask King Vlad to also send his personal thanks along with a token of his appreciation for their sacrifice. Have him assure the village that the menace has been destroyed and Dalca and Bogdan have received what they deserved for their actions."

"Well put, Doctor. You have not yet arrived at his castle but you have already done His Majesty great service." Then, as if in afterthought, she added, "As have you, Herr Morrow."

"What will become of Dalca and Bogdan?" Morrow asked. "At least they'll be spared the gallows tree."

Lady Alina and I exchanged glances.

"He doesn't understand, does he?" Lady Alina said.

"No, he doesn't. Should I tell him?"

"If you please, Doctor."

"Understand what?" Morrow asked.

"As in England, murder is a hanging offense. However, in Transylvania, there is a different penalty for treason. One more terrible than drawing and quartering."

A look of horror passed over the face of the werewolf as he realized what that penalty was. "Those poor bastards."

25

There are many castles associated with the being once known as Vlad Tepes of Wallachia, then Dracula and now Vlad, King of Transylvania. Castles Bran, Peonar, and Hunyadi are three of these, as is an unnamed structure on Mount Izvorul Călimanului, in the Calimani Alps. King Vlad does claim these as his own and has held court in all of them, but there is only one Castle Dracula and I was finally approaching it.

Perhaps the driver was told to arrive just as the night was giving way to the day, a time when the forces of light and darkness are briefly in balance. Perhaps it was by chance, but my first view of Dracula's main lair was by the light of the rising Sun. Even thus illuminated it was a dark, imposing sight.

Castle Dracula sat on a high, flat mountain. Sheer cliffs dropping several hundred feet protected it from the rear. In the front was a broad expanse of grass, a clear field of fire in the event of an attack. A forest ruled the rest of the grounds, broken only by a wide, paved road. I imagined that in the forest there were beasts that hunted both by day and night and so kept it free of intruders.

Looking up at the castle battlements, I saw artillery trained on the forest and the road. These were not modern guns or ancient cannons but tripod-mounted barrels that flashed red as they scanned the road for intruders. Above the castle soared Martian flyers, small delta-winged aircraft no doubt capable of resisting any attack from the air with lethal force.

As our carriage began its slow ascent the air grew colder, as if ignoring the warmth of the growing Sun. As we leveled off, I saw what I first took to branchless trees lining the road. These proved to be posts fixed into the ground, some topped with sharp points, others with rounded ends. I thought at first it was a reminder of King Vlad's history as *Voivode* of Wallachia but then I saw figures impaled on the two posts closest to the main gate. As we passed them, I recognized the features of Mihai Dalca and Darius Bogdan, their mouths opened in silent cries of pain and their sightless eyes crying tears of blood as they writhed in agony on their stakes.

Frederick Morrow was visibly shaken by this display. It was one thing to casually speak of such a thing, but to actually see it was another. I knew what he might be feeling. Though he was a king much loved by his subjects, Dracula was still the same monster who had fed on the crew of *Demeter* and sought to bring terror to London. Adding to my dismay, and possibly Morrow's, was the knowledge that he and I were in part responsible for the impalement of the two men since we had discovered their scheme and assisted in their arrest.

Morrow turned toward Lady Alina, the woman with whom he had spent a night of passion. His look asked the silent question of how she could be a party to such treatment even as he asked her, "How can they still be alive?"

"A few drops of blood from one of His Majesty's Brides will keep a man thus punished alive for a week, maybe longer," Lady Alina answered dispassionately. "Should they survive longer than a fortnight, they are removed from the stake."

"And what?" he asked. "Healed and pardoned?"

"Healed, yes. Pardoned, no. Their survival indicates that their life force is strong, so they are bled by the Brides who then feed His Majesty."

I will confess that if I had had my father's Webley with me, I may have been tempted to take it out and end Dalca's and Bogdan's suffering. I was not sure if I could have resisted the temptation. Although I did my best to remain stoic during the exchange between Morrow and Lady Alina, my face must have revealed my thoughts.

"How do you feel about this, Doctor Watson?" Lady Alina asked.

We were almost at the main gate when I answered.

"Dalca and Bogdan should have known the stakes, if you will forgive the expression, before they entered the game. As for their punishment, *pour encourager les autres, n'est-ce pas?*

"*Oui.*"

"Then why display them where no one can see them?"

I knew why. People arrive and leave the castle all the time, and so the word is spread. Better to have such things talked about than to be witnessed. Lesser cruelties than this had sparked revolutions.

Our carriage stopped before Lady Alina could reply, and so she was able to avoid my question with, "Ah, we are here."

At long last, I had arrived at Castle Dracula.

26

We were met at the door by an officious-looking man dressed in the finest of British butler livery.

"Welcome to Castle Dracula," he intoned. "Enter freely and of your own will."

And so we entered freely, met by what could only have been low-level renfields who fussed over us and tried to take our coats, bags, and anything else we chose to relinquish.

I surrendered my traveling bag but held on to my medical kit. With Morrow following one renfield and I another, we were escorted up the grand staircase. Morrow was taken to the second floor while I was led to the third.

The renfield opened the door to my rooms. "In here, if you please, Doctor Watson." Of course he would know my name. Dracula's minions are well trained.

I looked my escort over. He was an attractive young man, maybe fifteen, sixteen at the most, with a ruddy complexion, dark hair, dark haunted eyes, and a strong yet slender body. He was dressed in a scarlet shirt and black trousers, which I would later learn was the standard service uniform of the castle. I might have chosen a white shirt, but blood is less noticeable on scarlet.

"I have been assigned to you, Doctor. Please tell me if there is anything you need, want, or…desire." He looked pointedly at the bed making his meaning clear. One does not get that kind of service at the Savoy. Or maybe one does, I have never stayed there, although Holmes and I once solved a murder there, even if we never did determine what became of the clown.

"Thank you, er…what is your name?"

"I am Renfield, Doctor."

"As is every servant in this castle, I am sure. What is your first name?"

He looked confused. His eyes blinked several times, then rapidly moved back and forth as if he were trying to recover a lost memory. From his lips came a soft whisper, "I think I had one once," but then he straightened and said, "Just Renfield, Doctor."

Moving close to him, I looked deep into his beautiful eyes. There I saw pain, despair, and a desire to be free, or maybe it was just my imagination. I stepped back.

"I have to call you something." There was a boy once, a lost boy who, despite my best efforts, I was unable to save. "I'll call you 'Luca.' Would that be all right?"

"You may call me anything you wish, Doctor, at any time you wish, for anything you need."

Again, he looked at the bed. He might have been an enslaved thrall to a vampire king, but he was still a young man, and I fancy myself an attractive woman. But I have always been attracted to men older than he appeared to be. But even if I were inclined toward boys his age, or the type to take advantage of those who had no choice but to obey, I would hesitate to use this one in this place.

Again stepping close, I pulled back his collar to reveal the telltale signs of his having been bled. Still close, I slowly unbuttoned his shirt in a manner to suggest that I was yielding to the temptation of his young, strong body. Opening his shirt, I found that which I had been expecting, a barely healed wound on his chest from which Dracula had drunk his heart's blood. Again I looked into Luca's eyes. Was it he who looked back, or Vlad? Was the serpent even now watching to see if I'd be tempted by the forbidden fruit.

I stepped back, again looked at Luca, and saw something else I had been expecting. It was satisfying to my feminine ego to know that I was still capable of producing such a reaction in young men, or possibly old voyeurs.

Suddenly all business, I asked, "My luggage, my equipment, has it all been delivered and put away."

Shaking his head as if to dispel the cobwebs I had just put there, Luca said, "Yes, Doctor. Clothing in here, your equipment in the workroom."

"Thank you, Luca. I was expecting some communications. Did they arrive?"

"Yes, Doctor, telegrams. They are on your desk in the workroom."

"Again, thank you, Luca. There's just one more thing. Please bring something to eat. Something light for now and something more substantial around four."

"Yes, Doctor."

I barely had time to check my clothing and equipment before Luca returned with a cart. Again I thanked him by name, asking, "If I need you, how may I find you?"

"Just tell ask any servant that you wish your renfield, Doctor. And I have been told that you are to meet with His Majesty in the Grand Hall just after sunset. I will come and escort you."

"Thank you, Luca. Please convey my thanks to His Majesty and tell him that I look forward to meeting him in person."

With that, Luca left. I had decided to call him "Luca" every chance I had. If by doing so I could instill him a sense of identity, an idea that he was more than a nameless "renfield," that might be a small chink in Dracula's wall. It would only be one person, but sometimes one is all you need.

I ate my morning meal, then stared longingly at the bed. It looked comfortable. Sleep called but duty compelled me.

My rooms were in a corner of the castle, their windows giving me magnificent views of the Carpathian Mountains. Carefully peering down from my windows, I wondered at the sheer sides of the cliff on which the castle was built. I wondered if Jonathan Harker had made his escape in the way Stoker had said he had. But then Stoker was an author and not a journalist, and the former are permitted more lies than the latter.

It took me about an hour to assemble a small forensic laboratory in what Luca had called the workroom. It took another thirty minutes to install a quarter-ton deadbolt lock on my door. The lock would not prevent anyone from entering when I was out of the room but would prevent intruders from entering while I slept.

Again my bed called to me but messages from Holmes awaited me. I decoded them to learn that Fantômas had escaped from Strangeways Prison and had stolen the Ring of Gyges, that Thomas Capell was suspected of having aided and abetted him, and that I owed Holmes five pounds.

For the third time, my bed summoned me and after closing the deadbolt and setting my "Baby Ben" alarm clock, I yielded to its call

27

The clanging of the alarm clock woke me in time for Luca's arrival at 4:00. I thanked him, ate my light meal, then dressed for my presentation to the king.

Sunset, the second time in the day when the light and the dark are balanced. Only this time, instead of the dark giving way to the light it overcomes it. It is the time of dark things, the hours of the monsters. The old Scottish prayer came to mind as I dressed.

From ghoulies and ghosties
And long-leggedy beasties
And things that go bump in the night,
Good Lord, deliver me!

As I waited for Luca, I picked up my copy of Dracula to read what Stoker had to say about my host.

"His face was a strong--a very strong--aquiline, with high bridge of the thin nose and peculiarly arched nostrils; with lofty domed forehead, and hair growing scantily round the temples but profusely elsewhere. His eyebrows were very massive, almost meeting over the nose, and with bushy hair that seemed to curl in its own profusion. The mouth, so far as I could see it under the heavy moustache, was fixed and rather cruel-looking, with peculiarly sharp white teeth; these protruded over the lips, whose remarkable ruddiness showed astonishing vitality in a man of his years. For the rest, his ears were pale, and at the tops extremely pointed; the chin was broad and strong, and the cheeks firm though thin. The general effect was one of extraordinary pallor."

Before my departure, Holmes told me that this depiction, taken as it was from Jonathan Harker's journal, was fairly accurate, although the Dracula he had met and bested had appeared to be a much younger "man" than Harker and Stoker described.

Luca arrived. As he was to be my escort for the evening he had traded his red shirt for a white one and had added a black necktie and a coat. I was dressed in a Coco Chanel black dress that provided ease of movement while being long enough to conceal the silver-bladed dagger strapped to my inner thigh. The dagger with a blade of Damascus steel I carried openly, strapped to my waist, both a warning and a message to the ghoulies and ghosties. Let them see it, let them worry about it, let them take it if they dare. It will distract them from my true, unseen weapon.

The Great Hall was not that great, not when compared to the others I had been in. Those of Buckingham Palace and Windsor Castle were, of course, larger. Even the smaller halls of Thornfax and other manors and abbeys I had visited eclipsed the Great Hall of Dracula Castle.

Still, as in many things I have experienced, it is not the size but presentation that matters and the room into which Luca escorted me was simple and elegant with fine carpets from Turkey and tapestries illustrating the history of Transylvania and Wallachia hung on the wall side by side with those celebrating the long the life of King Vlad Dracula.

Only certain areas of Castle Dracula were equipped with electric lighting. The Great Hall was one of them. Despite this, that night the hall was lit by candles sufficient for one to see across the room but not so bright as to dispel the gloom from its corners room. What those dark corners hid I did not know but I prepared myself to deal with whatever might emerge from them.

There were perhaps twenty-five people in the room when the doors opened and Luca, in a clear and steady voice, announced "Presenting Doctor Jane Watson of Great Britain." He then withdrew. This was not as assemblage for such as he.

As one, the crowd turned. I saw the faces of some of my traveling companions among it–Sir Nigel, Herr Rosin, Sister Regis, Misters Falk and Lloyd. Neither Lady Alina nor any of the other renfields were present. As I said, this was not a gathering for the servants, however high placed or important to the king.

With all eyes on me, those assembled parted as if I were Moses and they the Red Sea. The path was now open to the king.

Conscious of the occasion, I slowly walked to the opposite side of the room where sat the king. On the throne's right was a contingent of his Carpathian Guard, all of whom were Romani descended from Danylo, father of the first Duke of the Rom.

To the left of the throne stood what I can only describe as the Vampire Council, creatures of blood and the night who had, willingly or not, sworn a blood oath of allegiance not to Vlad, King of Transylvania but rather to Dracula, Lord of the Undead. There were four whom I could see clearly and one who stood deep in the shadows. Of the four, I recognized two–Lord Aubrey Ruthven (who was of no relation to the Scottish Ruthvens of Freeland) and Sir Francis Varney (so much for the efficacy of throwing a vampire into a volcano). The others were unknown to me but I was sure that I would meet them soon.

Behind the throne, almost but not quite in the shadows, were three women. All had dark hair, one had dark skin. These, I was certain, were the current Brides of Dracula. They were looking not at the throne but at the king's Carpathian Guard.

In the center of this sat the king upon his throne. He appeared more dissolute than either Holmes or Stoker had described. His forehead was not as domed nor was his nose as thin. He was not as pale as I had expected and compared to the pallors of Ruthven and Varney, he was somewhat ruddy in complexion.

While Stoker's description may not have been accurate, he was a writer and so by definition a liar, I doubted very much if Holmes had been mistaken. Even so, when the man upon the throne presented his hand, I got down on one knee to kiss it. As I did, I pressed my finger onto his radial artery.

Quickly getting to my feet, I drew my steel dagger and placed it close to the left eye of the man on the throne.

"If you do not tell me where King Vlad is right now, I will pin your head to this throne then look for His Majesty myself."

The man's eyes shifted to his right, toward the Carpathian Guard. A quick glance showed me that in the center of the Guard was a man who fit Holmes's description of Vlad perfectly. In addition, the other members of the guard stood further apart from him than they did their fellows.

Sheathing my knife, I walked to this man. Stopping before him, I executed a precise bow, one deep enough for royalty but not as deep as the ones I have offered Kings George V and VI and King Edward VIII. (Incidentally, if the Brothers Holmes ever permit, I will one day relate the true story of the latter's abdication.)

Stepping away from his guard, most of whom were eyeing my dagger and no doubt recalling the speed with which I had drawn it, Vlad returned my bow in a kingly fashion then remarked,

"Most people would not dare to stand before a king armed such as you are."

Vlad's voice was hypnotic and amazingly like Bela Lugosi's although with not as much of an accent.

"I am not 'most people,' Your Highness. I am Jane Watson and I dare much. Besides, most monarchs do not possess your speed."

"That is true, Doctor. But the question is which of us is faster. Perhaps before you leave we will put that to the test." Vlad glanced toward the throne. On seeing the king looking at him the man sitting there quickly vacated it. "We do hope you did not frighten him too much. That is our favorite cushion. How did you discern the truth?"

"Your Majesty was accurately described by Sherlock Holmes. But I was not sure until I felt his pulse and found it beating much faster than yours would have. Besides, your Brides kept staring at you and not your stand-in."

"And if you had been wrong, Doctor Watson."

Then I would have killed as many as I could, beginning with you, is what I wanted to say. Instead, I sidestepped his question with "Why the charade, Your Majesty?"

"I would think the answer would be…elementary."

It was. It had been a test to see if I was as good as or maybe better than Sherlock Holmes. "What's good enough for *Jeanne d'Arc* is good enough for me. Now then, Your Majesty, I understand that you have a murder for me to solve."

"We do, Doctor, after dinner we will speak of it, just the two of us."

28

Dinner was in the room just off the Great Hall. Again, although the dining room was wired for electricity, it was lit with candles. The Council of Vampires did not attend. Neither did the Brides. They, no doubt, ate elsewhere. I tried not to think about what their meal might be.

King Vlad was in attendance, in his place at the head of the table. I was seated to his right. To the king's left was a giant of a man. His black hair was long and his face heavily scarred. I recognized him, for Holmes, having met him, had told me of him when he found the ten-year-old me reading a copy of Mary Shelley's book.

"Lies, Jane," he told me with a vehemence I've known him to use only toward utter villains, "Damnable lies."

"How do you know, Uncle?"

"I've been to Swiss caves and read the journals of Victor, Adam, and Elizabeth Frankenstein. Plus I have had the occasion to meet what Shelley calls 'The Monster.' I have encountered monsters–Roylett, Moriarty, The Sumatran Devil. Compared to them, Adam Frankenstein is no more a monster than you or I."

"You've met the Mon…the Creature, Uncle? Under what circumstances?"

"We first met when he asked me to find his son." Holmes waved his hand as if dismissing the matter. "A minor case, completed satisfactorily within forty-eight hours. As for that," he pointed to the book, "it was written by a ship's captain based on second, third, and even fourth-hand information." But when I moved to put it down he said, "Finish it by all means, if only to learn how valueless witness testimony can be. One day I will tell you the true story, when you are older, for it is not for the ears of one as young as yourself."

Among those guests at the table were my traveling companions. Each of us was attended by our renfields. Luca for me, young girls barely past puberty for all but Herr Rosin and the nuns. The latter had been collectively assigned older women, as was proper. Rosin was served by a young man not much older than Luca.

I was sure that these personal renfields had made the same offers to them as Luca had to me and I wondered if any had availed themselves of the offer. Possibly not Sir Nigel, I knew him and liked to think of him as a decent honorable man who would no more betray his wife than he would his country.

Rosin I was not sure about, although Dracula's choice of a male renfield revealed the vampire's knowledge of the German's personal tastes. Or maybe it was a guess or a temptation. As for Falk and Lloyd, the way they leered at the girls assigned to them made it clear that there was little need to tempt them.

Have they realized, I asked myself, *that their renfields were more than servants, that they were the thralls of Dracula, that he has access to their words, their passions in the night, the secrets they might whisper in the dark?* I resolved to have a discrete word with Sir Nigel. As for the others, they could go to the Devil.

Speaking of whom, or rather, his Transylvanian representative, he was a most gracious host. Addressing each of us, asking about our health, our lives, and our families. He even joined us in our meal, although his "wine" was redder and thicker than ours and he took but a few morsels of his food.

During a lull in the conversation, I talked across the table and addressed Frankenstein.

"Herr Frankenstein, it is good to meet you. My godfather, Sherlock Holmes, speaks well of you."

"Ah, you are that Doctor Watson, the daughter of Mister Holmes's friend and chronicler. Your godfather once did me a great service. And the world another…" Vlad cleared his throat and Adam's eyes twinkled as he changed his own topic. "How is he?"

"He is well. Older but still active."

Frankenstein's voice was quiet and gentle, if a bit rough. As we spoke, I experienced that *frisson* I had felt when I first met Lady Alina. That confirmed my suspicions about her. Just as I was wondering if Frankenstein felt as I did, he said, "There is something about you, Doctor. Perhaps we can speak later. I can usually be found in the King's library."

"You mean, your library, don't you, Adam," the king interjected. "You use it more than we do."

The two laughed the way good friends do and the conversation then moved on to other topics.

After dinner was over and the plates removed, King Vlad said, "Sir Nigel, Herr Rosin, we will see you both about three. Your renfields will bring you when we are ready. Use the time to familiarize yourself with the castle. But remember, this is an ancient castle. Not even we know all its secrets or its dangers. We warn you as your host, but we bear no responsibility as to what may happen should you wander about on your own.

"Mister Lloyd, Mister Falk, Lord Ruthven will be able to see you two within the hour. Please present your…proposals to him. Doctor Watson, we have some…personal business to attend to then we will be with you." Looking past me, King Vlad addressed Luca, "You," he said harshly, "you will bring your charge to us when we call. Is that clear?"

In a trembling voice, Luca replied, "Y…yes, Your Majesty."

"Good. In the meantime, show the doctor how to find the library."

29

I spent an hour perusing King Vlad's collection. One good thing about a long life is that it gives one a chance to accumulate a fine collection of books. The walls were lined with rare books, manuscripts, first folios of Shakespeare's plays, a Gutenberg Bible, and a section devoted entirely to various editions of Stoker's *Dracula*. There was also a shelf on which sat all of Holmes's monographs and other writings, including *The Practical Handbook of Bee Culture* and *The Whole Art of Detection*. Propped up against the latter was Moriarty's *The Dynamics of an Asteroid*. More ominously, there was a locked cabinet displaying various dark tomes and grimoires, such as *Les Cultes des Ghoules*, *Las Reglas De Ruina*, *The Book of Eibon*, and the most dangerous of them all, *The Necronomicon* and its companion volume, *The Ravings of el-Hazred*. Of the two, it is said that the latter is far more dangerous than the former.

As I pursued King Vlad's collection, I could not help but feel that I was being watched. Twice I turned to see if someone was behind me. But there was no one there when I did so. Each time I put my feeling down to my location. Castle Dracula seemed to have its own atmosphere, one that affected, and perhaps infected, one's mind and imagination. Still, it was entirely possible that Dracula had eyes watching everything all the time. Nothing so obvious as eyes moving behind portraits, but one can never be too sure.

As I was considering this, King Vlad entered the room. "There is a volume missing from that cabinet, Doctor." As he approached me, he placed a folder on a table. "It was stolen by Van Helsing when he invaded my home, butchered my brides, and slaughtered my retainers. Oh yes, Doctor, despite what is in that book," he pointed to the Dracula section, "I had attending servants the whole time Harker was here. It is absurd to think that I could maintain this castle on my own, or that I would lower myself to do.

"Van Helsing took only one thing, a volume compiled by the Golden Dawn…"

"*The Opening of the Way*," I said.

My interruption surprised him. "You have the book, you've read it?" he asked anxiously.

"I know of it, Your Majesty. It somehow came into the possession of…someone other than Van Helsing." I thought it best not to mention Helena Rossum's name or that she was now working for the British government. "The person opened a gate to somewhere else, a barren landscape where black suns cast dark shadows over creatures that should not exist. Fortunately, the gate was closed by Sherlock Holmes when he destroyed the book."

The king seemed pleased. "That is good. Van Helsing seeks to destroy all of what he regards as "unnatural creatures" such as myself, the were, even my friend Adam. He and his organization the Sway seek knowledge and artifacts that they believe will help them accomplish this goal. The book would have been a powerful weapon in this crusade of his. Tell your mentor that I am again in his debt."

"Again? Your Majesty."

"Yes, Doctor. Holmes could have killed me at Carfax Abbey as I lay helpless at his feet. Instead, he sent me home which allowed me to bring glory to Transylvania. He is the only man alive who has ever beaten me, or who would have spared my life when I was at his mercy. And speaking of debts…"

King Vlad reached into his pocket and drew out a small presentation box. He opened it to show a pendant in the shape of a dragon.

"This is the Crest of the Order of the Dragon. This one is for Sherlock Holmes." King Vlad reached into his other pocket and brought out a similar box. "And this is for you, Doctor Jane Watson, for your service to the King and Country of Transylvania in unmasking the two traitors who are impaled outside my gates and in bringing a murderer to justice. As well as the service you will do us in hopefully identifying another killer."

Taking my pendant from its box, he placed it around my neck. "Wear this while you are here, Lady Watson. It will mark you as a Knight of the Dragon. All who see it will know that to molest you is to molest us. And should they survive their encounter with you, they will not survive an encounter with us."

When a monarch, any monarch, grants you his favor and gives you a title, one can only bow and say, "Thank you, Your Majesty." This I did.

King Vlad bade me sit. "One of the privileges of the order is that you may sit in the presence of the king without waiting to be told." He retrieved his folder and sat next to me. "Don't worry about your renfield, we have sent him back to his quarters. He seemed unusually upset and his thoughts were troubled. Just what have you done to him?"

"I just showed some kindness, Your Majesty, that is all."

Vlad nodded. "Ah, that is it. The renfields of the castle, they are like children, no, rather they are like dogs. Pat their head, show them some compassion, and they attach themselves to you. Take care not to allow him to grow too attached to you for then you will have to take him with you when you leave, for he will be of no further use to me."

As if on cue, a large Dalmatian bitch walked into the library and sat at Vlad's side. He took the time to pet her and scratch behind her ears. She in turn looked up at him, her eyes filled with what could only be called love.

"This is Ella, Lady Watson, one of the few creatures on this earth who likes me for myself, and not for who or what I am or what I can do for or to them. She was a gift from my cousin in London, the one who lent me the use of her name to ship my coffins. But now, Lady Watson, let us speak of murder."

He sat across from me and opened the folder. "The victim is Mircalla, Countess Karstein of Styria. You may have known her as Carmilla, subject of a novel by Sheridan LeFanu, in which her death was, as was mine, greatly exaggerated."

"Why do you do it?" I asked. "Why have you and the others–Sir Varney, Lord Ruthven, and even Count Orlock, whom I assume was the one hiding in the shadows during my presentation, permitted Stoker, LeFanu, even Rymer and Prest to write novels about your kind?"

"You have said it, Lady Watson, they have written novels,

stories that are made up and so could not possibly be true. As Baudelaire has written, 'The greatest trick the Devil ever pulled was convincing the world he didn't exist.' By permitting these novels, we too convince the world that we do not exist. Some call us 'Dracula' and like you, know us for what we are. But most of the world knows us as Vlad, the king of Transylvania who keeps his people safe and makes the trains run on time." He said this calmly, proud of his great deception, his "Big Lie" as his soon-to-be German opponents would call it. My question answered in the way I thought it would be, I was ready to move our discussion back to the murder but Vlad went on.

"And before you ask, Lady Watson, yes, our subjects know of our true nature, and they are aware of the consequences of revealing it to outsiders. Nevertheless, they love their king, who has kept them safe and who will protect them throughout the coming war. They love us so much that our kind no longer has to hunt. They come to us willingly and consider it an honor to sustain the Council or my Brides. In exchange, they are cared for the three months they serve us. Some chosen few remain as renfields, others return home well rewarded for their contribution."

"Thank you, Your Majesty, I had wondered. But as you have said, let us speak of murder."

"Yes, let's. As we have said, the victim is Mircalla, the Countess Karnstein. Her body, what there was of it, was found outside the castle grounds just outside the woods. It had been exposed to sunlight but whether that was the cause of death, we'll leave for you to decide."

"Where is the body now, Your Majesty? Surely you did not leave it *in situ*."

"Of course not, Lady Watson. Alina had it photographed where it lay then moved to a level below the castle where it is cold enough that refrigeration is not needed. In the old days, we used to keep prisoners there. Now, it is a convenient place in which to store food and drink."

"And blood?"

Vlad shook his head. "Blood must be warm, and fresh, and

taken from the source."

From the file Vlad had handed me I took the photographs he had mentioned. They showed me how the victim lay but that was all. I'd have to examine the body.

"I'll need to inspect the scene. It has been preserved, has it not?"

Vlad nodded. "We have studied your father's writings as well as your mentor's book on detection along with Sir Sydney Smith's *Textbook of Forensic Medicine* and other such works. We knew how to proceed."

"I'll want to view the scene first thing after sunrise. And when we finish here I'll want to see the body. Has anyone been questioned in this matter, Your Majesty?"

"Yes, and no one admits seeing or doing anything. The renfields are, of course, in the clear. They are not permitted to harm any of my guests or allow them to come to harm. Should they do so, we will be aware of it and it would not be pleasant for them. One did once, about five years ago. Through negligence he caused one of my guests to be injured. He was five days on the stake. Since then the renfields have been very, very, diligent in their duties."

"I can imagine."

That was a lie. While I could imagine that Dracula's thralls were indeed very careful of his guests' comfort and safety, I could not imagine what they went through day after day, night after night, knowing that at any time, through no fault of their own, they may be subjected to the worst forms of torture at the hands of a monster.

"Is that all, Lady Watson?"

"Just one more question, Your Majesty. Why did you send for me? Why wait for over a week to investigate when there were investigators who were closer?"

"Closer, yes, but not as skilled. And we require the best. Now, you will forgive us, Lady Watson, we have other business." As King Vlad rose, so did I. Even with permission one does not sit when the king is standing. "Wait here. I'll have Darvell escort you to the lower levels. And, Lady Watson?"

"Yes, Your Majesty?"

"We are sure that one of the reasons you took on this commission was the opportunity to use your powers of observation to learn all that you can about our country and this castle. As our representative, you have free reign to go where you will. But beware, this castle is old, older than we are in fact, and there are places here not even *we* dare to tread, where dwell horrors that will not be impressed by that pendant we hung around your neck."

With that, he was gone and with it the feeling of having been watched. I left the library to get my medical bag from my quarters. When I returned, Augustus Darvell was waiting for me.

"Doctor Watson," he greeted me in a wavery voice. Then he saw the Crest at my neck. "Forgive me, Lady Watson. I had not known."

"No reason why you should have," I replied, "for it was just given to me."

Darvell appeared old, at least in his eighties, and I recognized him from the Great Hall. He was part of the Council of Vampires.

"You are Augustus Darvell, are you not, sir?"

"I am, Lady Watson. Please forgive my appearance. I came late to the undead life, if I may call it that," he said with a chuckle. "While it extended my life it did not restore my youth. Still, I have no cause to complain. That will come later, when the coldness of the lower chambers chills my ancient bones." Another chuckle. "Now then, please walk this way."

As I followed Darvell I saw that he did not move like the old man he appeared to be. I sensed an inner strength in him, one that I believed he tried to hide. I thought of Holmes, also in his eighties but with the vitality of a much younger man. Perhaps Darvell's aged appearance was a ruse designed to fool the unwary into underestimating him.

"Mr. Darvell, is there no way that your youth could be recovered?" I asked as we began to descend into the depths of the castle.

"There is, My Lady, one or two in fact. But my doing so would greatly displease Lord Dracula, and I have lived too long to end up with a stake in my heart, or one up my ass."

30

After being kept waiting for over an hour, Frederick Morrow was finally allowed his requested audience with King Vlad. When he entered the king's office His Majesty was alone, seated behind his desk. Morrow had expected that members of his guard to be present, ready to lay down their lives and to take his should he attack the king.

Approaching the king, Morrow gave a low bow, which His Majesty acknowledged with a nod. Morrow was not invited to sit. Indeed, there was no chair in which he could sit.

"Thank you for seeing me, Your Majesty."

"Skip the pleasantries, Herr Morrow. What do you want of us?"

"I am, as you are aware, what they call in this country a *vârcolac*, a werewolf. I have been for many years."

"And how did you come to this state?"

"I had been a woodsman, Your Majesty. There was this young woman, one who appeared to have just entered her teens. She had dark hair, blue eyes, and her cloak was red. When she asked me if I would escort her through the woods I agreed. When I suggested that we stop along the way, she agreed. I led her to a clearing that was suitable for the purpose. She undressed–her cloak, her blouse, her skirt. Then she changed–eyes, ears, teeth, fur. One minute a young girl, the next a ravenous beast. Like her, I had undressed but I kept my ax at hand. As she charged me I managed to strike her in the head but not before her claws scratched me and her teeth grazed me. Injured, she ran off. I ran in the direction from which I came. It was a full moon cycle before it became clear that she had passed her curse on to me."

King Vlad let loose a long sigh of boredom missed with angry indifference. "A story we have heard many times, Herr Morrow. You were lucky to survive and fortunate you have what is necessary in your blood to be able to turn. Not all can or do. It does not explain why you are here or why we should waste our time with you."

"If Your Majesty pleases. I will confess that, at first, I gave way to the beast within me. But soon I began to struggle against my bestial side. I wished to be rid of it. Then I heard the story of Peter of Epprath, known to some as Stumpf Peter. He is said to have used a belt to change from man to wolf to man again. I have also heard it said that you may have this belt. If so, I would do whatever Your Majesty asked of me if I could have this belt and be just a man again."

At first, the king said nothing, just sat and stared at the man-beast who stood in front of him. Then he shook his head and laughed. But his laughter was directed not against Frederick Morrow but rather the circumstance which brought him to this point at this time.

"A magic belt to change man into beast. Thor was said to have had a magic hammer, and Arthur a magic sword, and Aladdin had a magic lantern. They are stories, Herr Morrow, yet they are not. For there are items of power in this world. Some come from ancient times, and others come from Mars and beyond. As for the Devil's Belt, yes, we have it and other items like it. We hope to acquire more, not for our own use but to keep them safe lest their use destroys this world."

"So, Your Majesty, if you have the belt …"

"We see no reason to give it to you, Herr Morrow. As a man, it could easily be taken from you. As a man, you are of no use to us. We have men, men who would die for us. Men who would kill for us. What could you as a man do for us? What we need are monsters. Monsters like you and those to whom we have given sanctuary. We have gathered them into my land as the Valkyries gathered fallen heroes. And when the coming war starts and Transylvania is attacked, we will call on them to defend it."

The king let this sink in. Then, "Will you do that, Herr Morrow? Will you and the beast inside you defend this land, our land? If you will, then when the war is over we may let you try the belt. If not, then talk to our friend Adam. He has an elixir that will either kill you or cure you. Or else ask him where his father might be. Old Victor just might be able to give you a body free of the curse."

Frederick Morrow stood so long before King Vlad that the king raised an eyebrow. Finally, the man said, "I will fight for you, Your

Majesty, in the hopes that one day the belt will be mine."

King Vlad nodded. "Very well. You may remain at the castle until Doctor Watson completes her investigation. You will leave when she does. Until then you are our guest. As such you are to keep a tight rein on your other self. Infect anyone with your curse and you will be a long time on the stake. That is all."

31

The air three levels below was chilly but not freezing. This was good. I have thawed corpses before and it was not pleasant. At the door of the chamber to which Darvell had led me stood two of King Vlad's Carpathian Guard. As were the guards I had seen in the Great Hall, they were well equipped for trouble. They each carried a sidearm. On the opposite side of their pistol hung a scabbard in which was a short sword. Their uniforms were in the kings' black and red, and they each wore a black German-style helmet.

As Darvell and I approached they came to attention. On seeing my crest they saluted Roman style. Beginning to feel more important than I was, I reminded myself that what the king can award he can take back and that she who rises has further to fall.

I nodded my thanks to the guards. "Do either of you speak English?" I asked them.

"Legionary Dimitri, My Lady. I do."

"Good. To the best of your knowledge, Legionary, has anyone entered this chamber since the body of the Countess was placed inside."

"No one has, My Lady. As you can see, His Majesty's seal is intact."

Dimitri stepped back to show a large seal where the door and the frame came together. It bore the same design as did my crest.

"Do you know if anyone has tried to enter?"

"They have not, My Lady."

"How do you know this?"

"There is no blood on the ground."

"I am the Lady Jane Watson, Knight of the Dragon, and am here on the King's business. Please allow me to enter."

Dimitri said something to his partner. Together they again studied my crest. Dimitri then suddenly turned, drew his sword, cut the seal down its middle, and returned his blade to its scabbard. So fast was he that by the time I realized what he was doing he was done.

Dimitri's partner stood in front of Darvell and me, placing himself between us and the doorway. Once he was in place, Dimitri slowly opened the door. Both guards had their hands on their swords, ready to draw them should anything come rushing out. A wise precaution given what we were dealing with. On my part, I resolved to throw Darvell at any thing that attacked, reasoning that of the four of us, he had the best chance of survival, given that he was already dead, or, at least, the closest to it.

Other than the creaking of the door, nothing happened. With an audible sigh of relief, Dimitri stood aside to allow me to enter. Darvell moved to follow me but I stopped him.

"Mr. Darvell, would you please remain out here. Legionary Dimitri, would you please come inside with me as a trusted witness while your partner remains with Mr. Darvell?"

Dimitri said something in Romani to his partner, I suspected it was the equivalent to "Watch him." When his partner nodded, Dimitri turned to me and said, "As you wish, My Lady," and together we entered the chamber where lay the body of the Countess Karnstein.

There were no electric lights this far down. There were, however, sufficient candles for me to do my job.

The body was on a table in the center of the room. It was covered by a white sheet. Despite having been dead, if that term may be applied to a vampire, for over a week, there was no odor of decay. This was unusual. Even in a room chilled as this was, decomposition should have begun.

When I pulled back the sheet I discovered the reason for the lack of odor. The body was in a state of advanced decay. *So this is what a dead vampire looks like,* I thought. So few vampiric remains had been seen. Sir Varney was said to have been lost in a volcano. Lord Ruthven had never been brought to any kind of justice. Count Orlock was reported to have disappeared in a puff of smoke. Only the deaths of Lucy Westenra and the Lady Mircalla had been fully proved and documented, the first by Dr. John Seward and the other by Dr. Hesselius in his report on the finding of the Imperial Commission at Karnstein. The commission, at the urging of Baron Vordenburg, had exhumed her body and found it "immersed in blood, it's lungs breathing, its heart beating and its eyes open." They drove a stake through the vampire's heart and beheaded it. The body and head were then burned to ashes and the ashes thrown into a river.

Or so reported Dr. Hesselius and I have no cause to doubt him. Hesselius was one of the first, if not *the* first, investigator of occult and bizarre mysteries. In that, he was a contemporary and sometimes rival of Van Helsing.

Assuming that Hesselius's account was correct then it was impossible for the body that had been exhumed and cremated and the one on the table to be one and the same.

But which one? There is a belief, unproven due to lack of evidence, that when it suffers true death a vampire's body suffers rapid decomposition equivalent to the time of its true death. There was one way to prove this, but I doubted if King Vlad would permit me to kill one of his Council in the name of science. So I had only the corpse in front of me to go by.

"Send someone for paper bags," I instructed Dimitri. As he left to do so, I began my examination.

The victim was dressed, if that were the word for it, in a long, somewhat diaphanous dress that could have been either a scandalous evening gown or seductive bedroom attire. Either way, she was dressed to kill and had apparently gotten her wish, although not in the manner she had intended. There was no damage to the dress. She wore no jewelry nor did she have shoes. Her body lay flat, as if she had died in bed.

What I did not see was any sign of any heat injuries one would expect if she had been subjected to the deadly rays of the sun. The pugilistic attitude that bodies of burn victims exhibited was missing, and no charring of the remaining bone was observed.

I was beginning to suspect that any exposure to the sun was done post-mortem, that the victim had been killed inside then taken outside in the hopes that her death would be attributed to solar exposure.

Dimitri returned with paper bags and with his help I removed the dress. Our maneuvering of the body to accomplish this task caused us to work in close proximity and I began to think of other ways he might help me. I quickly put those ideas out of my head. While the Carpathian Guards were not renfields, they were strictly loyal to Dracula.

"Thank you, Legionary," I said when we were done.

"My pleasure, My Lady."

After thinking, *No, but it could have been,* I resumed my examination.

There was no evidence of wounds on the bone, not that any injury other than decapitation or extreme exsanguination would cause death. Silver poisoning would do so, and if I had successfully smuggled a silver blade into the castle others might also have done so.

There were no signs of silver that I could see, not even by extinguishing most of the candles and looking for traces of it with my torch. I thought of one other type of poisoning that might be lethal to her kind and so took samples of her stomach lining and from her mostly atrophied organs. Despite Stoker's claims, holy water and blessed objects had no effect on vampires.

There was blood in her stomach but not in the quantity I would have expected. It was as if her feeding had been interrupted. In support of this, I found traces of blood on her lips and in her mouth and throat. Possibly she had died while feeding. If so, then the blood might be that of her killer.

I had evidence enough to convict a murderer but there was still the tedious task of finding him, or her. Suspects would be questioned, motives explored, alibis checked, and vampires angered when I suggested that the killer may be one of their own. I hoped my Crest was the sigil the king said it was.

The remaining question was who the victim might be. Some years ago, Holmes had written an exhaustive monograph on the determination of the time of death of human remains. It was a fascinating work but one he dismissed as trivial and being of more interest to archaeologists than criminal investigators.

I recalled this monograph as I studied the remains before me. Based on Holmes's research, the body on the table in front of me was more likely to have suffered her first death about 50 to 75 years ago than 250 to 300.

Murdered she may have been, but this victim was not Mircalla, Countess Karnstein.

32

The next morning, as the sun rose over the castle and all good little vampires were supposedly comfortably in their coffins, I set out for the crime scene. I was accompanied by Luca who was carrying my crime scene bag. I had not yet been to sleep, having spent the rest of the night reviewing the results of the autopsy and preparing my report. King Vlad would likely require a report this evening. I did not want to displease him especially as there were things I needed from him.

His Majesty had been true to his word, the scene had been well protected. A tent had been erected over the area where the body had been discovered, and a trio of his Carpathian Guards stood watch. As there was no language common to us, I had Luca translate my words into Romani.

"You and your fellow legionnaires are to be commended for keeping this area safe and secure over the past week. You have my thanks and the thanks of Lord Dracula for doing so. When I am finished here today you may resume your normal duties." They looked relieved until I told them. "But I have one more important task for you."

This earned me the universal "what now?" look every soldier in every army has given more than once.

"Go with my assistant here. Form a line and search from here to the castle and back until you have covered as much ground as you can."

One of them asked Luca a question which he translated as "What the…(something) are we looking for?"

There was no need to ask what the "something" was. Some words need no translation.

I smiled and replied, "Anything that does not belong."

They left, three large men and one small youth, looking for that which might not be there, as I entered the crime scene.

Knowing what I would be doing that day, I wore women's pants, my silver dagger secured not too comfortably between my breasts, its strap hidden by that of my Dragon Crest. On hands and knees I searched the area covered by the tent, placing what I found into paper envelopes. When I was done searching it from front to back, I then searched from side to side.

My findings were few. The area being grass-covered, there were no shoe or footprints. There were a few threads that appeared to have come from the victim's gown. This was to be expected. There was also a button, dark in color, easily overlooked by anyone who had searched the scene standing up. There was a matching thread still on the button. If I were correct, the button had not been torn off, the victim being already dead, but perhaps it had somehow fallen off or gotten snagged. By such chance occurrences are crimes solved.

Judging by the sun, it was mid-morning when we finished. Neither Luca nor the guards had found anything. I had not expected them to but the search had to be made.

Before I dismissed the guards, I had one last question. Again with Luca translating,

"Gentlemen, you are the honored Carpathian Guards, chosen to protect the Lord Dracula as your fathers and their fathers have always done." They proudly straightened at this. "As such, you must know all the ways into and out of the castle, even the hidden ways. For how else may you fully protect your Lord?" Now they were looking suspiciously at me. "I do not ask what they are, but I do need to know if there are secret ways to enter and leave Castle Dracula." They hesitated. Why did the foreign woman want to know this?

Holding up my Crest, I said. "I ask this because it is important. I ask this as a Knight of the Dragon. I ask this in the name of King Vlad, Son of the Dragon and your Lord."

They came to attention, gave me the Roman salute, then began talking all at once. When they stopped Luca said, "There are several, known to but a trusted few. They regret they do not know where they are."

"Thank you, noble guards. When you are among your fellows, ask if anyone else has inquired about them. Bring the answer to me or my assistant and Dracula will reward you well."

We then returned to the castle. It was time for lunch, then a bath, and then a nap.

33

It was midafternoon when I awoke. Luca would be bringing me a proper tea at four. Again I reviewed my work. I had a theory but too few facts. By morning I hoped to know more.

Another message from Holmes. His telegram was cryptic, as it was meant to be. Numbers mixed with letters, words mixed with nonsense syllables. When translated it read,

"No records on Lloyd or Falk. Fugitives uncaught. M wants report."

Uncle Mycroft could wait. Code or not, I would be sending out nothing about Castle Dracula or its master until I was safely out of the country. King Vlad may have ways of telling lies from truths and if he asked, I wanted to say honestly that I had not betrayed his trust.

I had not expected Fantômas or Thomas Capell to be easily caught. The former's ability to be almost anyone made him as much of a ghost as his name suggested and one needs to know where an invisible man might be before one can hunt him.

I thought back to the affair at Thornfax Manor. It seemed that lately my life had been nothing but ghosts and phantoms. Fantômas, Griffin, Capell. Except that we had only the word of Griffin that Thomas Capell was, like him, an invisible. And only Moriarty's word that Griffin was still in her custody.

A coded telegram to Holmes.

"Verify Griffin. Why assume Capell?"

I would have Luca send it off after he brought my meal.

The news about the so-called arms dealers was interesting. As I wondered the how and why of their impersonation the very word triggered a thought. If one or both were not who they seemed, could one of them be Fantômas? Based on what I knew about the man behind the many disguises, one of them could be. But to what purpose? I imagined the master criminal attempting to fool Dracula, an attempt which could result in the story of Fantômas ending his days on a very sharp pole.

Luca arrived. He brought food and took away the telegram. After I ate, I changed into appropriate evening wear. As there were still some hours before the castle's main residents would be stirring, I decided to go to the library in hopes of finding a particular book.

34

This time I found the library without help or guidance from Luca. When I got there, I heard music playing from inside. Opening the door I saw Adam Frankenstein in a chair. He was reading Milton's *Paradise Lost*, holding the book with one hand and stroking a cat with the other. Behind him, a phonograph was playing an instrumental version of Irving Berlin's *Puttin' on the Ritz.*

Frankenstein looked up when I came in.

"If I'm disturbing you, Herr Frankenstein, I can come back."

He smiled. "Not at all, Doctor Watson. Do forgive my not rising. Fritz here hates to be disturbed."

Fritz was a mackerel tabby with almost as many scars as the man whose lap he occupied. On hearing his name he roused himself, looked first at Frankenstein and then at me. He mewed once then returned to his semi-somnolent state.

"Your cat?" I asked as I sat in a chair close to him and felt a now familiar tingle that seemed twice as strong as before..

"He seems to think so. The two of us have been together, well, ever since the beginning. We do lose track of each other but he always seems to find me."

"The beginning?"

"Of it all, my deaths and rebirth. Fritz was one of my father's first test subjects. In his journal, father wrote about killing a cat and returning it to life over and over. Soon the cat ran away. Fritz here is that cat."

"How you can be sure?"

"We children of the lightning can always tell when another is near. I feel it in Fritz and he feels it in me. And there's a little of it in you. I felt it last night. So Mr. Holmes shared his knowledge of the elixir with you?"

"Yes, he did, Herr Frankenstein."

"Please, Doctor, call me Adam. We are in some respect, distant cousins."

"Then I am Jane."

As I've mentioned, Adam Frankenstein's face was heavily scarred. To me, they did not make him ugly, but rather unique and I found myself attracted to it, and him. Perhaps it was the elixir but I began to wonder if the rest of him was scarred as well.

"Is Alina Renfield also a cousin, Adam?"

"You know she is, or you would not have asked. As I have my story, she has hers. I will let her tell it."

"And what is your story?" I dared to ask. "I've read Mary Shelley's book, but my godfather says it is far from the truth."

Adam laughed, and his laughter was as beautiful as his face was not. "That is putting it mildly, Jane. I met Shelley once. It was shortly after the second edition of her book came out. This time she put her name to it. She took fright when I appeared on her doorstep. Most people do, but her especially. Once she realized that I meant her no harm, she calmed. I then told her as much of the truth as I dared. In the end, we agreed there was nothing to be done. I left and never saw her again. As for my story…

"A part of me was a professor of natural sciences, a man who studied and taught about life and death. Another part of me was that man's assistant and servant. When both of these men were killed by the proverbial angry mob for a murder they did not commit, my father took the brain of one and the body of the other to create me. Displeased by his creation, he rejected me."

Adam held up his book. "Hence my fondness for Milton, for like Satan and Adam I have been cast out. Now I have become myth and monster, with few friends and fewer lovers." His eyes grew misty. "There was Henry, my friend. There was Elizabeth, who was Eve to my Adam. Now there is Holmes, and Fritz, and Dracula. Oh, I have no illusions as to his true nature but he knows what it is to be a monster, which is why he established a sanctuary for those like us.

"And that, in brief, is my story, Jane."

Reaching out, I took his hand. "I would like it, Adam, if you would consider me as your friend."

"Friend?" he asked and when he did I felt something more than the *frisson* caused by elixir. I think maybe he did as well for he smiled when I replied, "At least."

We enjoyed a silent moment until Fritz hissed, jumped from Adam's lap, and walked to the door. Adam followed, let him out, and closed the door.

"Will he be okay?" I asked.

Another laugh. "He is a hunter among hunters. The renfields avoid him, Count Orlock and Sir Francis are afraid of him. The others tolerate him because Dracula permits him to stay. He says that Fritz helps keep the rat population in check. But tell me, Jane. Did you come to the library with the hope of finding me here, or did you have another purpose?"

"Finding you was a pleasant surprise, Adam, but I came in the hopes of finding a copy of LeFanu's Carmilla and any related documents."

Adam pointed to a set of shelves in the back of the library. "Over there. Dracula has an extensive collection of works about his kind. He employs agents all through the world to seek them out."

Again he opened the door. "I shall leave you to your investigation. Good luck on discovering how the Lady Karnstein died."

"Thank you, Adam."

"Will I see you again, Jane?"

I smiled. "It is likely. The night is long and there is always the day."

He left. After some searching, I found the material I needed. I was ready for King Vlad.

35

They lived, or rather, they existed, in the crypts below that castle, where the dead of centuries past lay in their forever sleep. Some had been masters of the castle, others had been guests or opponents considered worthy of such an honor. The remains of former Brides were there as well, in the sepulcher carved out for them. Brides who had displeased the Master. Brides whom he had fully drained when he needed to increase his strength. Brides who had died when the Master still believed they could bear him an heir. In a place of honor were the Brides slaughtered by the one who had tried to destroy the Master. They had fought this Van Helsing and had cost him many men but he had prevailed. He had staked them and removed their heads and left their bodies for their master to find.

There were three, there was always three. Two of them were offerings from his people, the third the Master had brought from far to the south.

By day they slept. When the sun was gone they rose and left their crypt to attend the Master. Then they drank from the humans. When the sweet ecstasy of their feeding was complete, then the Master fed off them and the pain and pleasure of his teeth sinking into their bodies was even sweeter.

But of late, ever since the last visitors came, the whispers began. As the eldest lay in her stone tomb, as she awaited the time when she could arise, she heard a voice telling her that soon she would be sleeping with her sister Brides who were no more, that her Dark Lord and Master had chosen a new Bride, a young Bride. And that there could only be three and she was the oldest.

36

Before dinner, Luca brought me a message from one of the guards present during the examination of the crime scene. There had been no inquiries concerning the secret ways in and out of the castle. In one respect this was disappointing news. The identification of such a person would have led to a very viable suspect. On the other hand, it was now likely that the killer was one with knowledge of the secret ways of the castle.

Although the king was not present at dinner, his place was left open as was proper. Again the company was served by our renfields, none of whom looked physically damaged but there was a haunted look in the eyes of the youth assigned to Herr Rosin.

Without the king, it was a less formal gathering. Electric lights replaced candles. Adam engaged Frederick Morrow in conversation while I discussed religion with Sister Regis as her fellow nuns listened in silence. Lloyd and Falk sat apart, conversing with some of the other guests who were present–visiting merchants and ambassadors from Spain and Greece as well as representatives from other countries. None of these were involved in the events in which I found myself.

After the first course was served, I sent Luca with a note to the king requesting an audience later that night. He returned in time to serve the second course but appeared shaken and disturbed, his usually ruddy complexion paled. Although it is bad form to address servers during dinner I asked him, "Luca, what is the matter?"

He paused, then stammered, "It is nothing, My Lady."

I did not believe him but not wanting a scene simply said, "Wait on me after dinner."

His service after that was not exemplary but at least he did not drop or spill anything.

As I had instructed, Luca waited for me outside the dining hall.

"What happened to you, Luca. Were you attacked or injured?"

"I am, fine, My Lady. It is just that…His Majesty was with

the Council when I presented your note. They were feasting. The Brides… the Brides were there. They are…they are the worst of all."

Not caring what interpretations any who might have present might place on my actions, I pulled Luca into a mostly private alcove. Loosening his tie, I opened his shirt and examined his neck. No fresh wounds, only the scars left by King Vlad. I then had him take off his coat and pull up his sleeves. Again, nothing. I had to take his word that he had no new marks on the rest of his body.

"I will discuss this with the king when I see him. Which, by the way, is when?"

"At four, My Lady, but I beg you, do not mention this."

"Luca, you have been assigned to me. That puts you under my care and protection. No one but me or His Majesty may illtreat you. Now you may retire for the night. I will send for you if I need you."

Luca bowed and kissed my hand saying, "Thank you, My Lady." When he straightened, the fright I had seen in his eyes had been replaced by gratitude, as if for the first time someone had cared about him as a person.

Four o'clock was some hours off. I thought of returning to my rooms, but instead found my way to the Great Hall where most of the others had gathered. The Hall had music, and dancing, and cards. *Chemin de fer* and American stud poker seemed to be the favorite games of the evening.

I do not play cards or gamble at any game that is more skill than chance. Having been trained from an early age in the arts of deduction and observation I have an unfair advantage.

I do enjoy watching others play. It was my father rather than Holmes who said that one could learn much about a man by the way he plays cards.

There were five people at the poker table. Frederick Morrow, Joachim Rosin, Christopher Falk, Ambassador Jonathan Reid of the United States, and, surprisingly, Alina Renfield, whom I had not seen since my arrival.

Reid was an aggressive player, betting heavily when he was bluffing and even more when the cards fell in his favor. At first, he won but his winning dropped off once his fellow players figured out his game. Herr Rosin played like the German officer he was, advancing when his odds were good, withdrawing when they were not. Poker is a game of logic but also one of chance and bluff. Herr Rosin had the first but not the last and as for luck, she is a fickle lady who is only sometimes on your side. He lost more than he won.

Alina seemed to be playing only in her role as *de facto* hostess. She neither won nor lost.

Having witnessed Morrow's other self, it was clear to me that he was using his bestial senses to better "read" his opponents and thus improve his chances.

Falk was the most skilled. He was a virtuoso and the cards were his instrument and he won steadily. I was tempted to join the game just to see if I could beat him. A part of me wondered if I already had.

I was trying to decide if Morrow's use of his were-abilities was cheating or not when he gathered his winnings and excused himself from the table. With his departure, those remaining at the table switched to four-handed whist.

On seeing me, Morrow looked toward the orchestra and asked if I would care to dance. He was a graceful dancer and I followed his lead. As the music ended I asked, "How was your audience with the king?"

"Disappointing, Doctor, but not unexpected." Morrow led me to a table where we ordered drinks from a servant.

"It was odd, meeting a king alone like that. And he was every bit a king. He knew my nature yet did not have any guard with him."

"Given his nature, Mr. Morrow, I am certain there is little that frightens him. Besides, what made you think he was alone. Some castle walls are not as solid as they appear. A guard with a pistol or crossbow may have been concealed behind a secret panel."

"Not that you mention it, Doctor, I did sense a third presence, so someone may have been watching and listening."

Then he told me of his meeting and its outcome.

"So you believe that this 'Devil's Belt' can suppress your other self?"

He shrugged. "It's worth a try, not that I'll get the opportunity.

King Vlad's offer of my serving him in exchange for a maybe seems less and less appealing. But what choice do I have?"

I knew of one. "When this is over, should you find yourself in England, seek me out."

"You can help me?" he asked hopefully.

"I know some people." Although with MI-7 he might just be exchanging one devil for another.

Peter Stumpf's "Devil's Belt" reminded me of the Ring of Gyges, which, I reminded myself, supposedly had similar properties and had been stolen by a master of disguise who was assisted by an invisible man. As I've said before, Holmes may dislike coincidences but I've learned to heed them.

I did have a chance to consult with Sir Nigel. Taking him to one side, we stood facing a window as I explained the true nature of Vlad's minions and warned him of the dangers of getting too "close" to his young, attractive renfield.

"I know, Doctor," he said, looking into a darkness that was relieved only by the lights of nearby villages. "But a man gets… lonely and must sometimes seek comfort."

I was surprised at this confession. Sir Nigel was a gentleman of the old school, and as such would not normally even hint at such matters to a woman. Still, needs must and I was the only countryman in whom he could confide.

I briefly touched his shoulder. "Think of yourself as a priest, Sir Nigel, one serving God as well as King and Country. Be moderate as would befit a priest, and take comfort in your duty and, if need be, yourself."

If he was shocked by this advice he did not show it. "I will consider what you say, Doctor."

I thought it best to change the subject and so asked after his daughter.

"She's fine. Why do you ask?" He then added, "You must forgive me, Jane, but I have a meeting with Lord Ruthven and so must bid you *adieu*."

37

It was a quarter past four when I was admitted into King Vlad's office. It was dark, lit only by candles. There were no windows.

I could understand why Morrow had felt ill at ease. This was not the library, which was open to all. This office was Vlad's place of power, even more so than his throne. It was from here that he made the decisions that affected his country and possibly the world. And like him, I had the feeling that an unseen person was, if not present, then watching.

Even in the pale light, I observed that the king looked several years younger than when I had last seen him. There was a redness about his lips and a spot of crimson on his otherwise spotless white shirt. He had just fed and wanted me to know it. With a wide smile that displayed his extended canines he asked,

"What have you for us, Lady Watson?"

He was behind his desk. There were chairs against a side wall. I took one, placed it in front of his desk, and, as was my right, sat without invitation.

"If I may, Your Majesty, when one such as Lord Ruthven or the Countess Karnstein comes seeking your protection, how do you verify their identity?"

The King shrugged. "There is no need. Blood knows blood, by smell when they approach, and by taste when they submit."

"And do they submit voluntarily or after a struggle, symbolic or otherwise?"

Vlad leaned forward. "An excellent question. One we did not expect and which we would not ordinarily answer, but we suppose there is a purpose to it. It is the nature of beings such as us that we do not willingly yield except to one of greater power. So there is always a challenge. It is one of the mind and of the will. The stronger prevails and the weaker bares their throat. The weak one is drained and, should they recover, renewed by the victor's heart blood. We use them physically as well, to complete our domination over them."

"Your struggle with the Countess, was there much resistance?"

Vlad sat back, closed his eyes in remembrance. "She had not known a man, and that blood was very sweet. But otherwise, there was very little. We thought she would have been stronger. Ah, I begin to see what you suspect."

I place the book I had taken from the library—LeFanu's *Carmilla*. It was a first edition and illustrated. I opened the book to the page I had marked.

"And who is that?" the king asked when I pointed to a photo. Instead of answering, I produced the bound copy of Dr. Hesselius's of the finding of the Imperial Commission. I pointed to another picture. This one the king identified.

"That is Lady Mircalla, the Countess Karnstein."

"Forgive me, Your Majesty, but that is Bertha Spielsdorf, Lady Mircalla's victim before her assault and seduction of the Lady Laura, who, as you know, survived."

I then told the king of the exhumation and destruction of the true Countess Karnstein and of how I first came to suspect the victim's true identity. He considered this for a moment then shrugged.

"So she was a clever imposter whose reasons we will never know. She was still murdered while under our protection. How does this discovery bring us closer to her killer?"

"I do not know, Your Majesty. But consider, if there is one imposter in your midst, on your council, might there be others?"

Vlad sat back, thought for a time then, "We shall consider this. And while we thank you for this discovery we must ask, who killed her?"

"I think I know how she died—it was not by sunlight—and there are tests to be run." When I then told him what I needed for those tests he frowned and shook his head. For a moment I thought he'd refuse. But then he smiled his fang revealing grin again saying,

"They will not want to. They will resist. Which is reason enough to insist that they submit, to us and not to you, of course. Very well, they shall assemble in the dining room after dinner. You will not need the Brides, will you? One of them became quite agitated during our meal this evening. I'm afraid she tried to make your renfield her special treat and had to be restrained. I do hope he was not too upset."

"He will recover, Your Majesty. Thank you for your concern. I will tell him you asked after him. Your Brides are above suspicion as, of course, is Your Majesty. As for the others, I have met Augustus Darvell and have heard of Lord Ruthven, Sir Francis, and Count Orlock, but there was one other of whom I'm not familiar."

"That would be Boris Liatoukine. He was a Cossack officer who was betrayed by his men. They stripped him, exposed him to the elements, and left him for dead. He allowed himself to be turned to avoid freezing to death. After his conversion, he slew them all but did not feed on them. He's come to be known in his country as 'Captain Vampire,' even though he is now a major. He was sent as an ambassador by Premier Stalin but joined our council instead."

"And he has been here how long?"

"He arrived about a month before you…do you suspect him?"

"I must suspect everyone, Your Majesty."

"Of course you must. Anything else?"

"Yes, Christopher Falk is not who he says he is. At least, he is not Christopher Falk."

"We are aware of this. Falk is one of my overseas agents. As such, he travels incognito."

"And Peter Lloyd?"

"Window dressing, we suppose. Part of his disguise." The king rose, as did I. "Until tomorrow night then."

"Until tomorrow, Your Majesty." With a bow, I left his presence.

Adam was in the library when I returned the books.

"Your meeting went well?"

"Yes, it did." I told Adam of my discovery of the true identity of the murder victim and alluded to my meeting for the following night.

He smiled, his teeth much nicer than those of the king's. "That should be fun."

"For the king, I'm sure. As for me, I'll have angered the Council."

Adam pointed to the Dragon Crest. "But you'll have the protection of the king."

"I doubt if it will afford much protected against a maddened vampire."

"From what I've heard, it might. Plus, I'm sure you have your own resources."

I did, or believed I did. Based on one of my theories of the crime, I had prepared my steel dagger against such an assault. But being in the presence of Adam and feeling the *frisson* between us, I thought of a way to better prepare it.

"Adam, I must ask a favor." I told him what it was.

Another smile. "I can do that. I have it to spare. But I can do you one better but you will need to come to my room." He paused, waiting for my answer.

Adam Frankenstein was tall and strong, with long flowing hair and excellent teeth. His scarred face did not repeal me. Rather the opposite, I realized. And it had been some time since William. I agreed to meet him and, after a quick trip to my room for a certain personal device, I did.

Despite his size, in every respect of that word, Adam was a gentle, considerate, and adept lover. We spent an enjoyable couple of hours together and when we were spent, slept for several more.

When we awakened, Adam rose from the bed and walked over to a bureau. He was clad in only what God and Victor Frankenstein had provided and, yes, there were scars all his body. One day he would tell me how he came by them, and I would tell him of the few I carried, but that story is for another time and another place.

He took a vial from the top drawer of the bureau then turned to me. I had slipped out of bed and Adman watched me dressed as intently as he had when I undressed. He frowned as I hung my silver dagger between my breasts.

"That will get you staked."

"I cannot leave it in my room. I'm sure it's regularly searched. Besides, I feel as if I have already been staked, and very nicely too."

We both smiled at this, then he held up the vial.

"This is the true Elixir of Life, Jane, and not that seven-percent solution you and Holmes use. Be careful with it. It will save the life of a dying man, save it forever but at a terrible cost. And it will keep a dead man on this side of the veil until the spark of life awakens him and calls him back. It is not the blessing my father believed it would be. A forever life is not always a happy one."

I took the vial from his hand. "Thank you, Adam. For everything." We parted with a kiss that promised more to come.

38

The rest of the day seemed to pass quickly. But then, I had done little but eat, wash, sleep, eat again, and dress for the evening. And for those wondering, yes, it is difficult to prepare oneself when there are no mirrors. If ever again I visit a vampire's lair, I will be sure to bring a female companion, possibly Lady Molly of the Yard. Either that or request a female renfield.

With King Vlad presiding, dinner was again by candlelight. Perhaps, I thought, there was something about incandescent lighting that bothered the king and his kind. I wondered how bright an electric torch would have to be to have the same effect as sunlight. The image of angry villagers storming Castle Dracula with such torches in one hand and pitchforks in the other came to mind and I had to struggle to suppress a girlish giggle.

No one seemed to notice. It was a somber dinner. Except for any messages received by the ambassadors from their governments, there had been no general news from the outside since our arrival. For all any of us knew, the war may have already begun and we would be Dracula's guests for the duration. It was clear that the reality of being in a nest of vampires in the nowhere of the Carpathians was beginning to wear heavily on those at table.

As they had the night before, after dinner the guests dispersed, most to Great Hall to seek what diversions they could find. I remained in the dining hall waiting for the Council of Vampires.

They entered as a group, preceding their Lord. As one they sat, Dracula in the center of one long side of the table with Ruthven and Varney on his left and Darvell, Liatoukine, and Orlock on his right.

Ruthven and Darvell sat closest to the king. Liatoukine was seated next to Darvell, and Orlock next to him albeit at least a distance of two chairs, as if he did not want to be near the rest, or they did not want to be too close to him.

I could understand this, for if any living (more or less) creature resembled the devil it was Count Orlock. His skin was not just pale, it was white. His sunken eyes seemed to be two holes in his skull-like head. His ears were long and pointed. As for his mouth, his lips were perpetually drawn back, exposing a permanent predator's grimace.

Once the Council was in place, I sat, again without waiting for His Majesty's permission. I was not directly in front of the king, but rather as far to his left as would be considered proper, as far from Count Orlock as I could politely be.

Dracula began. "Gentlemen, we formally present to you Doctor Jane Watson, goddaughter of Sherlock Holmes, daughter of the eminent John H. Watson, and as you can, a newly appointed Knight of the Dragon. As such, and as our guest, she is under our protection, although we truly doubt if she needs it.

"Lady Watson, you have already met Mr. Darvell, May we now present to you Sir Francis Varney, Lord Aubrey Ruthven, Major Boris Liatoukine, and Count Orlock."

I rose and bowed, giving them their honors whether deserved or not. (Most likely not.) Darvell responded warmly, while greetings from the others were muted and unenthusiastic.

"Doctor Watson has come at our request to investigate the murder of one of our own. Already she has determined that she whom we believed to be the Countess Karnstein was instead an imposter and she suggests that there may be others in this council."

Thank you, Your Majesty, for putting me in the soup. While there was no reaction from Darvell and only worry on the face of Captain Vampire, Orlock hissed and, although I would not have believed it, his lips drew back even further and his eyes grew darker. I decided that if it came to a fight, he would be the first to die.

Varney's face grew dark as his eyes shot daggers at me. That was all right as I had one for him on my belt, and another more deadly strapped to my thigh. It was Ruthven who, half standing, openly objected.

"Your Majesty, I must protest. It is bad enough that we must meet thus, but to have this…mortal bitch suggest…"

"Enough, Ruthven." Dracula's voice was not loud but it had power enough to force Ruthven back in his chair. I now put Orlock second on my list as I imagined a blade of silver going through Ruthven's eye and into his brain. To me the king said,

"Lady Watson, on behalf of the Council we regret and apologize for the offense given you. Do you demand satisfaction?"

I looked at King Vlad. "Frequently, Your Majesty." I then looked toward Ruthven and lowered my eyes to where his lap should be. "But I doubt if Lord Ruthven could provide it." There was quiet laughter at Ruthven's expense and I considered the score even. "If it pleases Your Majesty, I would prefer that certain words be forgotten and that we continue our meeting."

Dracula nodded. "Well said, Lady Watson, as befits a Knight of the Dragon. Please, continue."

"To being with, I would ask Your Majesty to look closely at the members of your council."

"Why do you ask, Lady Watson?"

"I wish to know if any of them appear to you younger, stronger, or more vibrant than they were prior to the death of Bertha Speilsdorf? That is, in a way that could not be explained by their usual feeding."

The king smiled. "Ah, very good. we had not considered that. You do your mentor proud."

One by one he examined them, looking at their faces, possibly looking into what passed as their souls. Finally,

"There is nothing to indicate that they have fed off anything but what has been provided them. But, with the exception of Major Liatoukine, they are all old and wise and may be able to conceal what they have done, assuming that any of them are responsible. Pray continue, Lady Watson."

I hesitated before doing so, knowing how ill-received my request would be.

"Members of the Council, progress toward identifying the murderer has been made but there are tests to be performed. To that end, and to establish that you members of this council are genuine, I am requesting a vial of blood from each of you, to be taken directly from a vein."

There was almost another protest, this one more violent than the first. But then the king exerted his power over them. It was so strong that even I felt it. It lasted but a few minutes but when it passed the council was thoroughly dominated and I had resorted to calming myself with a mantra Holmes had learned in Tibet and had taught to me.

With the Council cowed, King Vlad addressed the council. "Let us rephrase Lady Watson's last statement. What she requests we now demand."

After that, I had no problem in obtaining a vial of blood from each of them. When I was done, I carefully packed them in my case and thanked them.

"Before you leave, Lady Watson, we must say in front of this council that we will require you to destroy whatever blood you do not use."

"Of course, Your Majesty. But instead of destroying it, I will place it in your hands to do whatever you deem fit with it."

"An excellent idea, Lady Watson. You may leave us now." Looking to his left at Varney and Ruthven, he pointedly asked, "Do you require a Carpathian Guard to escort you to your room?"

If I said "Yes" it might be taken as a sign of fear and weakness. A "No" could be considered foolish bravado. As the goddaughter of Sherlock Holmes and a Knight of the Dragon, the only thing I could say was, "Thank you, Your Majesty. But I believe I can manage on my own."

Of course, had it not been for Adam, and if the guard were Dimitri, I might have said "Yes."

39

Before the Master had met his council he had fed from her once again. When he was finished, the Bride descended to the resting place. The Master had drunk deep, perhaps punishing her for her attack on his slave. His feeding left her weak and when she begged him to call in one of his cattle so she could renew her strength and sleep untroubled by the hunger, he refused, leaving her in need.

The others were in their coffins, already lost in their dreamlike state. As she approached her coffin she heard whispers from the shadows.

"He meets with her, her and his council. He wants her to join with him, to become not just a Bride, but The Bride. A mortal woman who will bear The Child. He will then favor her with the Dark Kiss and become like him but not like you. She will sit at his side and you will serve her as well as him.

"But you can stop her, stop the one who has seduced your lord, your master, your lover. And I will show you how."

40

That night I had much to think about–the "haunting" of Thornfax Manor, the nature of Lloyd's and Falk's business with King Vlad, Frederick Morrow's conversation with the king, the feeling that we both had of being watched, and my conversation with Sir Nigel. Oddly enough, none of this had to do with the death of Bertha Spielsdorf. That I hoped to resolve that evening. The rest could wait until the following night, or so I thought. Unfortunately, while Holmes had the benefit of my father's advice, there was no one by my side to caution me against the dangers of overconfidence.

After my meeting with Dracula and the Council of Vampires, I retired to my rooms, not to sleep but to process the evidence I had gathered. After using my deadbolt to secure my door against visitors, I repaired to my spare room and began my work.

First I typed the blood I had obtained from the members of the council. When tested, none of the blood showed any reaction to the antigens. O-negative, then, on the face of it. But then I examined the blood samples under the microscope and found nothing but the virus cells that kept their undead bodies alive.

So vampires were not merely infected humans who needed blood to remain alive, they were creatures that had been transformed into something other than life as we knew it. This was groundbreaking but no one would believe it without proof. But I had given my word to destroy that proof on the conclusion of my investigation. No matter, the Brothers Holmes would believe me, as would the woman who once was Moriarty.

What was interesting was that when I tested the blood that I found in Spielsdorf's throat and on her lips, it proved to be A positive. Likewise that in her stomach. Her last meal was therefore not fully digested, indicating that she had died shortly after feeding.

If this were a mystery novel, or if I were a Belgian detective I would have suspected poison, and in a way I did. But what could poison a vampire? The virus seeks to preserve the body in its undead state so anything beyond the smallest amount of food and drink is usually violently expunged. But there was one substance to which I believed the virus was not immune.

On the table in front of me, I set up seven beakers. Into the first, I placed a sample of the blood I had recovered from Spielsdorf's lips. I then poured a small amount of the blood I had taken from each of the council members into the next five. I placed tissue I had removed from Spielsdorf's liver into the last

Then I took from its hiding place the vial Adam had given me. The Elixir of Life. Did I think about using it myself so I could live forever? Of course, how could I not? But was I willing to pay the price Adam had mentioned, having to harvest organs from the living to stay alive? Nothing was worth that. No. I would take what years were given to me and make the most of them.

I poured a measure of the elixir into the first beaker then stepped back. No reaction. I had not thought there would be. Then I poured the elixir into the next beaker. It was good that I again stepped back for there was an immediate and violent reaction that consumed both the blood and the elixir and shattered the beaker. It was the same with the remaining samples.

I knew then how Bertha Spielsdorf had died. And I believed I knew why. I used the elixir for one thing more then went to bed. In the morning when I woke, I would confront the killer.

Or so I thought.

41

Had she not hissed I would not have heard her. As it was, I awoke in time to grab what was under my pillow and throw myself out of bed just before she pounced.

I ran for the door. She moved to stop me. In the light of the lone candle I left lit I saw that it was a Bride, her hair uncombed, her eyes wild, her teeth exposed and sharp. She was dressed in a shift that was part nightgown and part wedding dress. She seemed weaker than she had been when I first saw her. She lunged at me and Lord she was quick. Only by luck did I escape her grasp but not without getting scratched by her claw-like nails.

My armed burned from my wound and I prayed I was not infected. But that was a worry for later. Right then, survival was my main concern. Before she could attack again I held up what I had taken from my pillow–not a cross as in the novels and movies, but the silver dagger given to me by Father Paul.

The Bride stopped. She knew my weapon for what it was, her true death should I strike her with it. Mine as well, if it were learned that I had brought such a lethal blade into the castle.

Now it was more than a matter of my escape. It was a fight to the death, hers or mine. Slowly I moved my dagger through the air, catching and keeping her eyes as they followed the shiny blade. I backed toward the dresser where I had left my other dagger to dry. She mirrored my movement, stepping forward as I stepped back, being careful not to come within reach of my deadly knife, waiting for a lapse of attention that would allow her to disarm me, possibly literally, and drink my blood.

She hissed and moved forward. I thrust with my dagger and she backed away. Yes, she could have overcome me but not before being pierced by my blade. She was not so crazed as to want my death at the cost of her own.

My rear hit the dresser. With my eyes locked on the Bride's, I reached behind. I touched first the Damascus steel, then felt for the hilt. Grasping it firmly, I brought it round.

Now it was my two blades against a vampire only slightly less deadly than Dracula and we were in stalemate. Even in what I presumed to be a weakened state she was still the stronger and I did not doubt that she could outwait me. That is, she could if not for the dawn. She would make her move before then for when the sun rose she had to be abed.

On my part, I did not know if I could maintain our standoff. My arms were getting tired, especially the one she had scratched, the one that held the coated, steel dagger. I had little time in which to make my move.

When Houdini was teaching me the arts of magic and escape he always emphasized the value of distraction. "When you are doing your magic, have them look someplace else," he told me. So distraction it was.

Again I waved the silver dagger, then I flipped it into the air. As her eyes automatically followed it, I rammed my steel blade, coated as it was with the Elixir of Life, into her left eye. I thrust forward and buried it in her skull.

Her scream was loud enough to have awakened the castle. Only thick, stone walls prevented this. Those who did hear probably assumed that some unfortunate had met their end. But even with a knife in her eye, the Bride did not go down. She still came after me and had it not been for my skill in *baritisu* she might have caught me. As it was, I dodged her and she struck the wall. Quickly getting behind her, I grabbed her head and smashed it into the stone wall, driving the knife deeper. Only then did she go limp.

I stood over her until I was sure was truly dead. She decayed only slightly, from a young girl almost in her twenties to that of a woman in her fifties. Convinced that she would not rise to attack me, I ran to my workroom and poured the elixir over my wound. The reaction of the elixir to whatever was in my arm stung badly at first, then got worse. There was burning as I had never felt before but when it passed the wound was closed, leaving only a scar that I would carry for the rest of my days.

Once healed (or so I hoped) I retrieved my silver dagger from where it fell. I then pulled my steel one from the head of the Bride, cleaned it off, and again coated it with the few drops of the elixir that remained in the vial. Not wanting to receive the inevitable visitors in my nightclothes, I dressed. With one blade at my side and the other strapped to my thigh, I opened the door to my rooms and found the renfield who attended the floor.

"Find His Majesty. Tell him that Lady Jane Watson requests his presence in her rooms."

"I…I cannot do that, My Lady," she protested. "It would be worth my life if I disturb His Majesty."

"It will be worth your life if you don't. Find the king and tell him that he's in need of another Bride."

It was only when I was back in my room that I remembered that in leaving it I did not have to unbolt my door, that the latch had already been pulled back. I realized the implications of this just as the king arrived.

To say that Dracula was not pleased would be an understatement. When he saw the body of his Bride his face lost its semblance of humanity and the beast within him emerged.

"Who has done this?" he snarled.

I took a step back, my hand on the hilt of my dagger ready to draw it and use it, committing regicide and probably plunging Transylvania into civil war.

"I did. She attacked me."

This surprised him and caused him to pause long enough to calm down as he considered the fact that a mortal had fought and killed a vampire almost as powerful as he.

"How? Why?" he asked once he regained control of himself.

"How, Your Majesty? Viciously. Why?" I shrugged. "When I find the one who gave her entry into my room I will ask him."

"You know who he is?"

"I know what he is, Your Majesty, and I think I know how to expose him." I said this even knowing that I might be warning my quarry.

"Then do so, Doctor, and do so quickly. You were brought here to solve a killing, not to cause one."

"She left me no choice, Your Majesty."

"Agreed. A loss, but she can be replaced." He then smiled, "Lord Ruthven and Sir Francis will be more respectful of you now." He looked down at the now dead Bride. "We will give orders to have this removed and the floor cleaned. Afterward, you can get what sleep you can."

42

Renfields came and removed the body. Again I was alone in my rooms. Or believed I was. No matter. If he had wanted to kill me himself I would now be dead.

I did not want to sleep, not with so much to do. Find the killer. Identify the imposters. Locate what was hidden. Instead, I stood at the window, looking out into the dark and listening to the creatures of the night. A bat may nor may not have flown by. It was just a bat. As far as was known, being changed into a flying rodent was not one of the effects of the virus. After all, unlike Frederick Morrow's affliction, there was the conservation of mass to consider.

Morrow. His reason for coming to Castle Dracula tied into what was happening. Stumpf Peter's belt, the Gyges ring, both were said to cause or cure a state of change. And the king collected such objects. For the common good, or so he told Morrow. Perhaps he believed the legends, that these were items of power. And why not? How long ago was it that invaders from space were merely stories as well. Now tripods and airships with death-dealing rays are a part of life. Why not rings and belts made up of a substance that alters the human body? I thought of Morrow and Griffin, one changed by infection and the other by science gone wrong. Both victims of the abyss that forever seems to swirl around us.

Again I thought of Morrow. I used him once, in the affair at the Borgo Inn. I could use him again. Since my bolometer was back in London, I would have to.

The sun rose, shining across the mountains. The castle would be quiet until it left us once more. My bed looked inviting but no. There was, however, a chair. I sat, intending to rest for just a moment.

There was knocking and cries of "My Lady, My Lady." I woke confused and disoriented. When I realized where I was and how I got there, I reached for the blade at my side and unlocked the door. It was only Luca.

"Oh My Lady," he sighed in relief and ran to me, stopping just before he embraced me. In my state I would have permitted it, even welcomed it but he, at least, knew his place and it was not with his arms around me. "My Lady, I am glad to see that you are safe." Pausing, he looked around the room, looked at the bloodstain on the carpet. "It is said that you fought and killed a Bride." There was wonder and admiration, and maybe a little fear, in his voice.

"I did."

"Was it, that Bride, the one who almost attacked me?"

"I believe it was, Luca."

"Was it, was it because of me?"

What to tell him? If I said "Yes" that might have made it murder for revenge. But I could not tell him "No."

"I do not know why she attacked me, Luca, But I can tell you that knowing what she tried to do to you helped give me the strength to defeat her."

This time he did embrace me. "Thank you, My Lady." Then he got down on one knee and would not rise. Thinking, *Oh Lord, what have I done*, I lifted him up.

"How may I serve you, My Lady?"

It was ten o'clock by my Baby Ben and my stomach was telling me that I was hungry. But business first.

"Find Frederick Morrow and tell him that I require his presence on the King's business. When he arrives, I will want breakfast for two. If he's not in his room try Lady Alina's." (Luca did not seem as shocked by this as I thought he might.) "If he's not there, hunt up his renfield and ask her."

Luca left and sooner than I had thought returned with both Morrow and enough breakfast to feed several people.

Like Mycroft Holmes, I did not like to discuss business while I ate. So it was some time before I told him why I had summoned him.

"So, Luca tells me you killed a Bride," he asked over what was now a very empty table.

I nodded and pointed to the stained carpet. "Right over there."

"I know, I smelled the blood when I came in. Now, why did you send for me?"

"I need you." He looked toward my bed and smiled. "Not like that. Besides, I've heard you bite." He did not deny it. "When you told me about your meeting with King Vlad, you said you had had the impression of being watched."

"Yes."

"As did I when I met with him. Herr Morrow, your senses are more acute than mine. Your impression of being watched, have you felt it since?'

He thought a minute then, "Yes, I have, Doctor. Every so often I catch a whiff…ah! Then how did you…"

"The king's office is not that big. Close quarters and a trained awareness, perhaps." I pointed to my door. "That was latched, yet someone entered through it. Now while vampires may be able to descend a sheer wall facedown they cannot dissolve into mist and reform. The latch was thrown from the inside. I need to know if he was here, Mr. Morrow. Can you tell?"

"Maybe." He stood up from the table. Addressing Luca, who had been attending us, he said, "You may want to leave, Renfield."

"My name is Luca, Sir, and I will stay with my lady."

Morrow grinned, his mouth full of sharp teeth. "Brave boy."

Morrow changed just enough to do what he had to do. He grew hairier, his face narrowed and his nose became snout-like. As he began sniffing around the room, Luca moved close to me, in front of me, actually. I think if Morrow went to the bad, Luca might have thrown himself in front of him to give me the time I needed to take the beast down. As Morrow had said, he was a brave boy. Or rather, a brave young man.

Murrow had my scent and from an appropriate distance took Luca's. He then bent low to the stain, sniffed at it, then shook himself as if he had smelled something foul. He sniffed at the latch and around the room in general. He spent about ten minutes in my workroom. When he came out he had resumed his human aspect.

"Luca, if you will be so kind and if your lady permits, I could use a glass of wine. No, wait, last night in the Great Hall I remember seeing a bottle of Irish, Tulmore Dew I believe it was. If you can, bring me the bottle."

Luca looked at me and left at my nod. "Well?" I asked.

"You, the boy, His Majesty, the vampire bitch. How many removed the body?"

"Two."

"Then them and one other. The other's scent was also in your workroom. Speaking of which, any chance you could whip something up that will cure me?"

I shook my head. "Perhaps, but most likely it will kill you."

"Doctor, there were times when I would have risked it. Those mornings when I woke up bloody and naked with no idea of where I'd been or what I'd killed. And those nights when I had to slip out of whatever town I was in just ahead of angry people who had figured me out. But that was decades ago, before I learned to control the beast inside. But even now, at home, and never mind where that is, I keep a silver knife against the time I again wake up bloody and naked."

It was then Luca returned, a half-full bottle of Jameson's in his hand. "It was all they had," he explained.

"It will do, and thank you, Luca. But Doctor, as I was about to say, the other's scent was in your room and I think but could not swear that it was his scent in the king's office."

"Find him for me, Morrow. Find him for the king who will no doubt be most grateful."

"Probably not grateful enough, Doctor. But for you, I'll find him. And when I do, you'll have to tell me more about those people you know."

Morrow left and Adam came in. On seeing his size and scars Luca moved to leave.

"Please stay, Luca. I might need protection."

The young man tensed then saw me smiling and relaxed.

"I heard you were attacked," Adam said. "Obviously, you are all right. What happened. The story I heard was not exactly credible."

"If the story was that I killed a Bride it was the correct one."

For the second time in as many days, I surprised Adam. (Never mind the first time. That is none of your business.)

"Why? How?"

A very popular question that.

"Why? She attacked me. How? I have you to thank for that." I told him about coating my steel blade with the elixir.

"So that works," he said. "I always wondered if it would. But that means…you don't think..?"

I told him what I suspected.

"Vlad is not going to like that. What if he tries to take his anger out on you?"

"He can take his trinket back. And if he further objects, well, I've been wondering about the combined effect of the elixir on a different kind of blade."

"I know a way out if it comes to that."

"I thought you might. But I have work to do. Before you leave, I think there's still some breakfast left."

Adam looked over at the remains on the table.

"Thank you, Jane. But I've eaten already and don't enjoy sausages."

Saying, "Fortunately I do," I gave him a certain look and was pleased to see Victor Frankenstein's creation blush.

After a mutual promise to meet later that day, Adam left.

"Luca," I said, "please find me Legionary Dimitri." When he left, I bolted my door against intrusion and thought about rings and belts and invisible men and those who had other ways to make themselves unseen.

There was a loud knock followed by a "My Lady." The voice was that of Dimitri. When I opened the door he gave me a Roman salute and said,

"Your renfield stated that you needed me."

"Thank you for coming, Legionary. Yes, I do. Could you arrange to have a flyer take me to the Cluj-Napoca Aerodrome?"

He hesitated. "A…flyer, Lady Watson?"

"Yes, Legionary. One of the aircraft that protect this castle. I assume there are more than two of them. I need to go to the aerodrome and return before the sun sets. It is on His Majesty's behalf that I ask this. It refers in part to the business of last night."

"I have heard of that…business, My Lady. We of the guard did not think it possible to do what you did and are most impressed. So impressed that we will be giving you extra attention when you attend His Majesty."

Warning delivered and received, I thought. "I understand your concern, Legionary. And it is in its own way a compliment. But rest assured, I am His Majesty's guest and he is my client and for those reasons I do not and will not seek to harm him."

"Then we understand each other, My Lady. As it is on the king's business, I will have someone meet you here within the hour to escort you to the roof.

An hour later, I was airborne in a ship Mycroft would have paid a king's ransom to have delivered to Harmondsworth.

The arrival of one of His Majesty's flyers at Cluj-Napoca created a stir. Despite being notified in advance, tripods turned their deadly light cannons our way until our pilot signaled all clear and correct.

We were met by a delegation of the aerodrome's staff and headed by its manager. I told him the reason I was there. As I was dressed in a manner befitting the king's emissary, wore the pendant that marked me as a Knight of the Dragon, and was flanked by two Carpathian Guards armed with sword and pistol he was quick to direct me to the proper office.

My business did not take long. When it was complete, I had what I come for.

"Legionaries," I said to my guards, "I could not help but notice that there are some fine shops and restaurants here. Would either of you object to a good meal followed by say, two hours of free time?"

Neither did. We had a late lunch then parted. I had to visit two jewelers before finding one who could do the work I needed.

We were seen off by another delegation who were most pleased with my promise to commend them to His Majesty for their service. On the way back I looked over the documents I had obtained–the passenger manifest of the Carpathian for the day of my arrival, the aerodrome's records of arrival for that same day, the hotel's guest registry. They helped confirm what I had expected.

43

When I returned I summoned Luca and had him deliver the message that I would not be in attendance at dinner that evening. Most would assume that it was because of the previous night's incident. If that were the case, I would let them. On his return, I gave Luca further instructions. Shortly after he left Adam arrived. A very sweet hour later I explained that it would not do for both of us to be absent from the evening's meal. On his departure, I put on my best skulking clothes. When Luca returned with his report as to who was at table in the dining hall I too left my room.

To prepare me for the life I was to lead, Holmes had arranged for me to be taught by a number of trainers. One of them was an American fighter pilot who had been shot down behind enemy lines and had spent the rest of the Great War making things miserable for the Germans. Not only did he teach me how to fly but he taught me the art of concealment. An art that I understand he put to great use when he returned to New York.

And so, knowing this night might come, I had studied the shadows of the castle. Where they were the darkest and what clothing would blend with them the best.

Dressed in the darkest grey and wearing a thin, black, hooded cloak I became one with the darkness and easily avoided the renfields as they went about their business. I roamed the halls and burgled the rooms. Fortunately for me, none of the doors could be locked from the outside nor did any of the hinges squeak.

Herr Rosin's room first. With a hooded torch, I searched his quarters. There was evidence that he shared his bed with his renfield but nothing to suggest that he was other than what he appeared to be, a representative of Hitler's Germany. Still, some of the papers I found that proved his allegiance bore information that would interest Uncle Mycroft and so I committed what I could to memory.

I felt a pang of guilt in searching Sir Nigel's chambers and some disappointment when I did. Like Herr Rosin's, his bed had been recently used by two, probably just before his going down to dinner. Not only had he broken the vow he had made to his wife but now he was compromised and would have to be recalled, assuming he was Sir Nigel. While I had found nothing to indicate that he was not, neither had I found proof positive that he was.

The search of Lloyd and Falk's rooms turned up nothing other than they were posing as arms dealers or possibly were arms dealers using pseudonyms to conceal the discovery of their activities by British officials. As they had previously indicated to me, their notebooks showed dealings with Russia, Germany, Italy, and several of the Balkan countries. Records of British arms manufacturing and purchases were also included. For some, especially merchants of death, impending war is good for business. But King Vlad knew of their impostures and called them his agents. Could it be that they were gathering this information to help Vlad determine how strong the forces were that might stand against him? Even if this were so, it did not exclude the possibility that one of them was an even greater imposter.

There was one more suite of rooms to search, for form's sake if nothing else. I expected nothing to come of it. As I came up on the rooms, a light appeared from under the door. Of course, they would have retired early, forgoing the festivities after dinner. I would have to leave this search for later.

Another light under another door appeared as I stealthily made my way back to my rooms. As I knew this room to be vacant, I silently approached it and, steel dagger in hand, carefully opened the door.

It was the bed that first drew my attention. There was nothing to be seen on it except a wooden stake. It was standing uptight, its point invisible. Blood was slowly leaking from the point where the stake disappeared.

Having seen this, I turned to the one who had turned on the light. Frederick Morrow stood in the corner. As his eyes darted between me and the unseen body on the bed he said,

"Well, Doctor, I found your invisible man."

44

In his novel, Mr. Wells wrote that upon the death of the Invisible Man his body gradually became visible. Although based on the truth, Mr. Well's story was fiction in that Griffin had survived and was now reportedly in the custody of MI-7. So unless Moriarty had killed him, Capell, or one like them to observe the result, no one knew what happened when an invisible died.

Except that now I did.

Nothing. An hour after I had found Morrow with the body it was still invisible.

"How did you find him?" I asked right after he announced himself.

"Once I knew what I was searching for, I started catching whiffs of him throughout the castle. Soon though, I found a place where his scent was strong and followed it as it got stronger. The trail led me to this room. There was no doubt that he was in here. It was dark when I walked in so I switched on the light and there he was. Then you walked in."

I wasn't sure if I believed him or not. After all, of everyone in the castle, only Morrow had the ability to sniff out an invisible man, or so I believed. As for his arriving in the room just before I did, I had only his word for that. He could have killed him in the dark and either waited or left and came back. But…why?

If Holmes's report was right, an invisible man helped Fantômas to escape in exchange for his stealing the Ring of Gyges. But Fantômas betrayed him as he had so many others. Why? Because, like the scorpion, it is his nature. But also because he knew that he would be hunted. He needed to get out of England and he needed funds. Being the man he was, he knew that Dracula would be a willing buyer for the ring. So in disguise, he boarded the *Carpathian*. The invisible man followed him and somehow stole the ring back. Morrow found out about the ring, thought it would have the same properties as Stumpf Peter's belt and killed him for it.

Except, how did Morrow find out about the ring and where would he expect an invisible man to be hiding it on his naked body?

I decided to believe Morrow. Besides, I needed his help.

"Turn off the lights," I told him.

"Are we just leaving him here?"

"No, Herr Morrow, we are not. For what I have to do darkness works better. And I do not want any passersby to question, as I did, why there is a light in an unoccupied room."

The lights went out and for the third time since leaving England, I was examining a dead body.

I had observed only a small amount of blood around the stake in the chest. Had the stake been the cause of death there would have been more. And so, in the dark, free from the distraction of trying to view a body I could not see, I let my hands examine the victim. Ventral side first–feet, calves, knees, thighs, and so on up to the neck. There my fingers felt evidence that a ligature, a flat, thin cord of some kind, had cut deeply into the neck. The head was next. I had expected to feel a familiar facial structure, Griffin or Thomas Capell. But it was neither. This was a third invisible man. And where there were three…

Certain things became clear but before I decided how to act on them there was a surface examination to complete.

Leaving the stake in place, I rolled the body on its side for a dorsal examination. No wounds save that the stake had fully penetrated the body, partly pinning it to the bed.

In answer to my question as to where on his body an invisible man might hide something, I found evidence of a non-sexual violation of the anal cavity, possibly post-mortem, although it was impossible to be certain without a visual examination. (The things I do for King and Country.)

The vacant room was on the cliffside. Anything put out of the window would no doubt be forever lost, especially something that could not be seen. The secret shared by the victim, Fantômas, me, and one other would be safe.

I should have done it. For King and Country, I should have done it. If Dracula learned or even suspected that the British government had invisible spies, it might push him closer to the Axis, or at least further from Britain.

I should have done it. Mycroft would have encouraged me to do it, may have even commended me for prompt action. Holmes might have been disappointed but would (probably) have understood. But dammit, he, as much as my father and mother, had raised me to do the right thing and so I was not about to unceremoniously throw a man who had died in the service of his country into the great darkness.

True, the dead man had tried to kill me but he had believed it was for King and Country. For that, he deserved justice, or at least vengeance.

"Herr Morrow, would you please go out into the hallway and ask a renfield to summon a legionary?"

"Yes, Doctor."

He returned with Dimitri and one other.

"My Lady, when I heard it was you I had to respond."

Without comment, I stepped aside to allow him to enter. When he saw what was on the bed he at first did not understand. Slowly the truth dawned on him.

"I have not read Wells's book but I have seen the film. I had not thought such a thing possible," He looked at the stake. "Was he a vampire as well?"

"No, Legionary. The stake is just…window dressing. The real cause of death was strangulation." I indicated where he should put his hand to feel the ligature mark.

"The killer was a coward then. You, My Lady, would have killed him with your hands, or your blade, for allowing the Bride into your room."

Legionary Dimitri was smart. With some training, he could solve the next mystery at Castle Dracula himself.

"What do you need me for, Lady Watson?"

"I will need a guard on this door until such time I can return here with the king. If anyone but me or His Majesty tries to enter, prevent them using all necessary force."

In answer Dimitri gave me a Roman salute, saying, "It will be as you wish, My Lady."

"Thank you, Legionary."

We left the room. He and his fellow took their place at the door.

By the time I returned to my room and cleaned up, making sure to give my hands a more than thorough scrubbing, the night was almost over. Luca brought breakfast and left with instructions. Then it was time for sleep.

45

When I awoke I dressed and, with my forensic bag, returned to where the body of the invisible man lay. It was still invisible, the bloody end of the stake seeming to hover over the bed. With the candles lit and the remaining sunlight coming through the window, I was able to conduct the search that was not possible the night before.

The surface of the stake was too rough for fingerprints. The furniture drawers were empty. The floor was devoid of any hairs and fibers from which to make Holmes-like deductions. There were small spatters caused by the ramming of the stake into the body, some on the bedclothes, some of which appeared to float in the air but were really on the body.

Given the circumstances under which the crime was committed, it was one of the cleanest scenes I had been on. The killer had been very careful not to leave anything behind. But there was another part of Edmond Locard's theory and I was counting on the second part.

46

As I left the room I thanked the two guards standing watch for their continued service and told them that their detail should not last much longer. Then I sent Luca to find Adam. He was, as I had suspected, in the library.

"Adam?"

"Yes, Jane?"

"Have you met the nuns?"

"Just in passing. I have not spoken with them."

"Good. Would you please send them a message asking to meet with you here?"

"Why would I want to do that?"

"Because you are a soulless creature who is now searching for a path to God."

"Jane Watson, I'll have you know that I am a Catholic."

"Since when?"

"Christmas Day, 1901, baptized in Rome by Pope Leo XIII himself."

"Well, that explains your repeated use of the phrase 'Oh God!' Then tell them you're tired of eating fish on Friday and want to be an Anglican. Just get all three of them here and don't let them leave."

"You haven't answered my question, Jane?"

"Call it unfinished business. I have to search their rooms."

Leaving Adam to his task, I went to the nuns' rooms and searched that. Their spare habits hanging in the wardrobe appeared to have been freshly laundered. Too bad, not that minute bloodstains would be easy to see on dark robes.

There was a double bed in the main room and another in the spare. I assumed Sister Regis slept apart in the latter and Sisters Miriam and Teresa the former. Or not. Perhaps one of them snored.

My search of the room turned up nothing. No evidence of murder, no torn leather strap, nothing to indicate that the nuns were anything except the brides of Christ they claimed to be.

I opened the shutters and, like Adam had not too long ago, looked past the courtyard at the stakes. The bodies of Dalca and Bogdan were still there, although they were no longer writhing. Seeing this made me think that soon theirs would not be the only bodies to be so impaled.

Finished, I went to see the king who was already waiting for me when I arrived in his office. As soon as I was seated before him he asked,

"What news have you for us, Lady Watson?"

"I know how Bertha Spielsdorf died, and why." At this the king sat up then leaned forward, his cold eyes blazing in anticipation.

"But first I must beg Your Majesty's indulgence. There is another matter that may be of greater importance than the one for which you commissioned me."

Frowning, his eyes grew dark again and his canines, usually hidden, began to emerge.

"Doctor Watson, we cannot imagine a greater matter than the murder of one under our protection, even if she was not whom we believed her to be."

"There is a dead, invisible man in one of your unused bedrooms."

That got his attention. "If he is invisible, how do you know he's dead, or even there?"

"Would Your Majesty care to see for himself, so to speak?"

His Majesty would and soon, accompanied by two of his Carpathian Guards who, as promised, kept a closer watch on me than they did the king. Soon the king was staring at an apparently floating stake and verifying for himself that it was firmly planted in an unseen body.

"We have read Mr. Well's book. Is this, or rather, was this Griffin?"

"It is not, Your Majesty. I once...encountered Griffin. This is not he."

"How does this connect with the death you were brought here to investigate?"

Instead of answering, I asked. "The Ring of Gyges, has Fantômas delivered it yet?"

"Yes… how did you know? Never mind, you would not be the goddaughter of Sherlock Holmes if you did not. But let us not discuss that here."

47

We were back in the king's office. He chased his guards out with, "Find out where the body of the dead Bride was taken and retrieve her ring. It will be needed for the new Bride."

They left and we were alone.

"The ring was delivered the day before your arrival, Lady Watson. The payment was made by a telegraphic transfer of funds."

"No doubt, Your Majesty, to an account which no longer exists."

King Vlad smiled. "No doubt. From all accounts, this Fantômas is a clever man."

"That he is. Would Your Majesty care to describe him for me?"

Dracula smiled, then he laughed in a way that suggested that he knew a joke and could not wait to tell it.

"There is no need, Lady Watson, for you saw him yourself when you were presented at court."

I had seen many people then, but which one could it have been. Then I got the joke.

"Damn it. It was he on the throne impersonating Your Majesty."

Nodding, the king laughed again. "Yes, he came into our office disguised as us. After our business was conducted he mentioned that it might be amusing if he impersonated us during your presentation. But now, he could be anyone."

No, not anyone, for he had arrived on the *Carpathia*.

"May we remind you, Lady Watson, that, like you, Fantômas is a guest in this castle. As such, he is under my protection. You may take no action against him except in self-defense."

"And if he should abuse Your Majesty's hospitality?"

"That would be a different matter. What do you believe he may have done?"

"I suspect him of killing the invisible man."

Vlad shook his head. "An uninvited man who was not under my protection. And as you well know, suspicion is not proof. If it were, many of Sherlock Holmes's clients would have been hung."

I changed my tactics. "May I assume that once Your Majesty obtained the Ring of Gyges, it was placed in the vault with the other artifacts."

"Yes, we placed it there ourselves. And in answer to your next question, the location of the vault is known only to us, and we were not followed."

"Given the existence of an invisible man, is Your Majesty certain about that?"

The king thought about my question for a few moments then realized the implications.

"Damn. Remain here, Lady Watson." Then he was gone. Shortly after, a member of the guard came in and placed what I supposed was the deceased Bride's wedding ring on the king's desk. It was of onyx, a sharp contrast to the traditional gold ring.

While waiting on the king's return I reflected on how rings kept playing a part in this case, two cases really, beginning with Thornfax Manor. The ring of Gyges, both then and now. The rings worn by the newlyweds. The ring Sir Nigel had tarnished by breaking his wedding vows. The ring of the Bride of Dracula.

It was then that I not only knew how to find Fantômas but the Ring of Gyges as well.

48

It was an enraged Dracula who returned to his office. His face as red as it would ever get, his eyes were almost black with fury, and his lips were parted and his teeth bared. I sat still and remained silent and hoped that he would not take his anger out on me.

As I was weighing my chances of mortal combat against the Lord of Vampires, the king slowly calmed himself. Still, he was almost growling as he said,

"It is gone, as is the Devil's Belt. It was that werewolf. He wanted it. When I refused, he stole it."

"How?" I asked quietly. "He does not know where it was hidden."

"He was in league with that invisible man. The belt for one, the ring for the other." He was about to the guard to take Frederick Morrow into custody when I said,

"I know where the ring and the belt are, and who has them."

"Where are they, Doctor?"

"Unless Adam has failed me, they are in the library."

49

When we arrived at the library Sister Regis was arguing with Adam.

"You can't keep us here."

"I can and I will, Sister. I am acting on the orders of Lady Jane Watson, Knight of the Dragon and representative of King Vlad himself."

"That will be all, Adam."

Adam smiled when he saw the king standing in the doorway. The three nuns, however, did not look pleased.

"Adam," Dracula said, "Please step back."

Right where I would have put him. The nuns were now between us and him.

"Lady Watson, if you would."

One never really looks at nuns. You see their habits, their wimples, their veils. But unless you are talking to them, you never see their faces.

I had spoken with Sister Regis but not to Sisters Miriam and Teresa. Now I studied their faces. He could have been either one.

"Sisters," I said, "as Brides of Christ you wear wedding rings. Please remove them and place them on the table."

Miriam obeyed right away. Sister Teresa was hesitant. I drew my dagger.

"I will have that ring. Whether you keep your finger is up to you."

With Dracula in front and Frankenstein behind, Teresa had little choice. She removed the ring.

Miriam's ring was a plain band on both sides. As she wore it, Teresa's ring also appeared plain but only because she wore it in reverse so as not to expose the mounted red ruby to view. On examining it I saw that the inside of the ring bore an inscription in an unknown language. I held it up to King Vlad.

"This was the property of an Oxford Professor of the English

Language who donated it to the British Museum. It was stolen from there by Fantômas. Nevertheless, Your Majesty, I believe it would be safest with you." I handed it to him. "I would, however, ask Your Majesty to take better care of it this time."

"We will, Doctor," Vlad said dryly. "As to the other?"

I studied the faces of the two in front of me. Teresa now looked even more nervous than before. Miriam was calm. Teresa then.

Knife in hand, I slowly approached Teresa with what I hoped was an evil grin on my face. "I will have the truth."

She broke. "No, it was him, he made me do it. He made me wear that ring."

She pointed to the one known as Miriam. Seeing the game was up, Fantômas dropped all pretext of being a *religieux*. He tested Dracula's speed and made for the door. He failed. As King Vlad held him tight, I cut the habit from him. Around his waist, I found a shaving kit along with the Devil's Belt.

"Good work, Doctor Watson, even if you do seem to be solving every mystery save for the one for which you were brought here." To Fantômas he said, "You, sir, have killed someone living under our roof."

"Forgive me, Your Majesty," Fantômas said calmly. "But I do not believe there is proof that I have killed anyone." He may have been exposed but he was going to play his cards the best he could.

But we were playing Dracula's game, and in that game, the king is always the highest card.

"If Lady Jane were to examine the strap around your neck, the one from which hangs the cross you bear, would she find it a match for the one that strangled the invisible? But about his death, we do not care. He was here uninvited and so deserved whatever happened to him. You, however, have abused our hospitality by stealing from us."

But Fantômas was not yet done and said calmly, "Your Majesty, I retrieved these items from the invisible man, whose name I never knew. I was going to return them to you at the proper time."

The was an iciness as cold as the grave in the king's voice when he said, "The proper time was as soon as they were in your possession. The proper time does not involve concealing the belt or suborning someone else into wearing the ring. You have betrayed us and for that, the penalty is the stake."

Fantômas then turned to me. Perhaps he was going to ask me to intercede for him. I hardened my heart and cut off whatever he was going to say with a shake of my head.

"Monsieur Fantômas," the king said, "it occurs to us that you have a great wealth of knowledge which it would be to our benefit to learn." On hearing this, Fantômas relaxed even as I inwardly cursed. It seemed as if he was again going to escape his just punishment. Then his hopes were dashed.

"However, as you are a proven liar, we are afraid that we will have to subject you to methods that are rigorous and very painful. And when we are finished with you, when we have, if you will pardon my expression, drained you all that you know, only then will we consider your final fate. There are worse things than impalement and perhaps what is left of you will beg for the mercy of the stake. And if we are then in a forgiving mood, we may grant you that mercy. Guards!"

Two members of the Carpathian Guard appeared almost immediately. "Take this away," King Vlad said. "Put it somewhere dark, cold, and wet."

Dracula then turned to Sisters Regis and Teresa. "Are you really nuns?"

"No," Regis said, "He hired us. Or rather, he hired me. I hired Teresa. She's mostly innocent of all of this."

"Mostly innocent," the king mused. "Very well. Teresa, or whatever your name is. Tonight you will serve us." His extended fangs left no doubt as to what form this service would take. "It has been too long since I directly drank from a neck as lovely as yours. Tomorrow, you will be held in solitary confinement until the coach returns to take you all back. As for you, Regis…"

"Your Majesty, if I may?"

"Go ahead, Doctor Watson."

"Teresa, who slept in the single bed?"

"I did," she said quietly.

"They were lovers?"

"Yes, and partners as well. She knew of the ring he made me wear and the belt that he wore. How could she not?"

I had only wished for the king to know the full extent of her culpability when I asked. If I had known what his sentence was going to be I might have remained silent.

When we left his office, King Vlad had placed the onyx ring in his pocket. Now he produced it. "I am in need of a new Bride," he said coldly. "You, Regis, shall replace her. Teresa, I will not be needing you tonight. It is, after all, my wedding night."

Again King Vlad called for his guards. As the screaming Regis was led away in terror, the king closed the door of the library.

"Now then, Doctor, we think it is time that you revealed just who killed Bertha Spielsdorf."

50

We met in my room. Adam was with me, Luca stood outside the door and admitted Alina when she arrived.

We were seated at my table, with Adam at my side and Alina across from me. The *frisson* I normally felt when I was with one of them was now more than doubled.

"You wished to see me, Lady Watson?"

"Yes, Alina. Or would you prefer Justine?"

Alina stared at Adam in anger. "Why did you tell her?"

"I did not," he said calmly. "Jane is a very good detective, remember? As soon as we meet she deduced that you and I were cousins of a sort."

"I suspected your nature even before I met Adam," I said, not bothering to explain the how or why to her. "Your slight Swiss accent told me who you might be. My meeting with Adam only confirmed it. Tell me, Justine, or Alina if you prefer, how did you come to Castle Dracula?"

There was a pause then she closed her eyes and thought back to an earlier time, a time when she had a family of sorts and a happier life.

"I was nurse to William Frankenstein, Victor's bother," she said, "His mother left him in my care. Poor William. He was murdered. They blamed me for his death and sentenced me to death.

"I remember the steps to the scaffold, and the hood over my head, and the rope around my neck. I remember the prayers of the false priest, the one who had lied about me. I remember the drop. Then, nothing. I died that day.

"But I awoke reborn from that nothing. And like a newborn I was naked. Victor Frankenstein was there, as was his friend Henry Clerval.

"Neither touched me, not in that way. Instead, they told me that they had redeemed me from the darkness. They gave me clothing and money and told me that the woman I was, Justine Moritz, was dead and that I should take another name and seek another life.

"And so I did. For almost a hundred years I wandered, not growing older, doing whatever I must to get by. Finally, I found my way to this castle. King Vlad took me in and I willingly became his servant."

"When he met you, did the king sense the elixir inside you?"

"He must have sensed…something, for he did not make me his own. Or else it pleased him to have someone who served him of her own free will. It was he who named me Alina. It was I who took the name Renfield to signify my loyalty to him."

In my pocket, I had the button I had found at the site where Bertha's body had been found. I took it out.

"Alina," I said, "if I were to search your rooms, would I find an article of clothing that matches this button and thread? And if I take a blood sample from you and compare it to that I found on the lips of the woman known as the Countess Karnstein, what would it show?"

Again she was quiet. Finally, "We were lovers," Alina quietly admitted, "almost from the day we met. I had been in service for just a few months when she arrived. Despite her nature, she was gentle with me. She never drank blood from me, nor I her."

"You did not drink…blood. But other fluids excited you both, did they not? She enjoyed the slight taste of true life, you were thrilled by just the opposite. Then came that last night when she lost control."

"No!" Alina shouted in denial. "She was alive when I left for Cluj-Napoca."

"So you probably told people. But the aerodrome hotel's records show that you did not arrive until the night before the *Carpathian's* arrival. After the murder had been committed."

To this she had nothing to say.

"Alina, the mark of the vampire does not quickly fade away. Please show me your neck."

"The mark is not on my neck," she said quietly, a sudden blush coming to her face.

"I see. Adam, would you please turn away?"

"There is no need," she said," there are no secrets between us."

I felt an unreasonable touch of jealousy and forced myself not to turn and look at Adam as Alina stood and raised her skirt. The mark was on her left femoral artery. It was faded and almost healed but it was there.

"When I felt her teeth I tried to stop her but she bit hard and deep. When she started drinking, the pleasure was so great that I no longer cared what might happen. I knew the elixir would keep me alive but I didn't know it would kill her. But after only a minute or two she pulled away from me. She screamed once then collapsed. Soon she was like you found her."

"Why did you not tell King Vlad?" Adam asked. "He would have understood."

There were tears in Alina's eyes. "He *might* have understood. But he might have seen someone whose blood could kill a vampire as a threat. Worse, he might have used me as a weapon against those of his kind who displeased him, offering me as a special treat then smiling as his enemy withered before him. And there was the shadow of the stake, an everlasting life of impalement. And so I waited until daylight. Using one of the secret ways, I carried her as far into the woods as I could. I did not expect the king to send for you."

"Is that why you tried to have me killed?" I asked harshly then continued over her denial of "What? No."

"Is that why you suborned the invisible man to let a Bride into my rooms, a Bride you had somehow maddened against me?"

Through her tears, I could see the confusion on her face. "No, I didn't. I couldn't. Bertha was an accident. To seek your death would be murder."

"How did you know your lover's name was Bertha Spielsdorf and not Mircalla?"

Sudden silence, then, hesitantly, "She told me."

"No, she did not. She would not. She was an imposter and you were loyal to King Vlad. As your affair progressed you went to the library to learn more about her. There you learned the truth. What then, Alina? Did you let her know that you knew? Is that why, during your last time together, she tried to kill you by draining you?"

There was no expression in her voice when Alina said, "She was angry. We fought. She made me promise not to tell anyone. When I agreed that's when…it happened. It *was* an accident."

"No, it was not," came a voice from the doorway to my workroom.

It was the king. He had been in my workroom, listening to my questioning of Alina. Now he emerged.

He came into the room and stood next to her, the lights in the room casting his shadow over her. For a moment I thought he would snap her neck and but for her nature, he may have. Instead, in a voice mixed with sadness, disappointment, and anger he said,

"Your first duty was to us and not to your lover. You should have told us of Spielsdorf's impersonation as soon as you learned of it. Your failure to do was a betrayal. And for that there can be only one penalty."

Everyone in the room knew what that was. Knew of the stakes beyond the castle gates where the traitors and other criminals were impaled.

There were times during his career when Sherlock Holmes would ignore, bend, or even break the law in the interest of justice. There were also times, such The Case of the Amateur Cracksman, when he wished he could have but was constrained by circumstances.

"Those are the hardest, Jane, and they are ever with you. And if you cannot do what might be required of you, abandon crime and stay with medicine."

Only now did I understand him.

"Alina Renfield. Having betrayed us and our Kingdom of Transylvania, we sentence you to…"

"If I may, Your Majesty?"

Dracula turned and looked at me. His features were stoic, his face unreadable. "You have identified the killer, Doctor. Your task here is done." He looked back at Alina. "The rest falls to us."

"Your Majesty, when you left Transylvania to lead the combined forces that defeated the Martians, did not Alina Renfield ably manage your affairs here and effectively run not only your castle but in part your country. She could have betrayed you then, for power and profit, but she did not. And did she not help expose the schemes of Mihai Dalca and Darius Bogdan when they attempted to rob your subjects. And when Alina went to the Cluj-Napoca aerodrome, it would have been an easy matter for her to book passage on the *Carpathian* and beg refuge in England in exchange for revealing all she knew of your affairs. But she did not. No, she returned to you. Even knowing who I was and why I may have been summoned, she remained loyal to you and returned."

Pausing, I looked at the king whose face remained passive, giving no hint as to whether my pleas had moved him. Nevertheless, I went on.

"Yes, she failed you by not revealing the true identity of Bertha Spielsrdorf. But to do so would have meant betraying the one she loved. She was trapped between duty and love, and so, not suspecting the tragic accident that her choice would lead to, she chose love.

"I believe that in the past you have loved. Justina and Ilona, these were your true brides. Remember your feelings toward them and you will know how Alina felt. And if after all this, you cannot bring yourself to show mercy but insist on sentencing your mostly loyal servant to an eternity of pain on the stake, you can have this back." Slowly I removed the Crest of the Dragon and placed it on the table in front of me. "For while I am honored to be a Knight of the Dragon, I will not be the knight of a monster."

There was a deathly silence in the room when I finished my appeal. I had already dropped my hand to my side in the hope that I could reach the silver blade strapped to my thigh before Dracula reached me. I was plotting my escape from the castle when King Vlad spoke.

"There is much of what you say, Doctor. But how do I explain the death of Bertha Spielsrdorf?"

Adam spoke up. "Blame Fantômas, or the invisible man. Or do not explain. A king need not explain anything. Simply tell the Council that the matter has been settled to your satisfaction and do so in a way that leaves them worried as to which one of them will be next."

Moving away from Alina, Dracula motioned for Adam and me

to rise, then sat in my place across from her.

Picking up the crest, he handed it back to me.

"This is yours, Doctor." I took it from him but did not put it on. To Alina he said,

"We have decided that you do not deserve the stake. However, the fact remains that you still betrayed us and for that you must be punished. There are dungeons below. They are cold, wet, and dark. You will be taken to one of them where you will remain, alone and without food or drink, until such time as you are freed. Is that understood?"

Alina bowed her head. "Yes, Your Majesty. Thank you, Your Majesty."

Then he turned to Adam and me and when he asked us, "Do you two understand?" a hint of a smile played about his mouth.

"We understand, Your Majesty," Adam and I said as one.

After Alina was led away the king said, "Doctor, if you will pack up your clothing and equipment we will see to it that it is taken to Cluj-Napoca for transport to England. Your coach will leave overmorrow. If we do not see you again you have our thanks, for everything."

I put the crest back on and bowed. "You are most welcome, Your Majesty."

51

Adam and I spent that night and most of the following day making love and plans.

The night before I was to leave, I left him sleeping in my bed and again donned my skulking clothes. As I readied myself to leave Adam awoke.

"Are you sure you do not wish me to come with you?"

"As I recall you did that not too long ago. As for accompanying me, you were not built for stealthy work."

I leaned over and kissed him. "You know what to do if I do not return."

"I do."

I picked up my bag and left the room.

Relying on my memory of the route I had taken with Augustus Darvell, I descended to the lower levels of the castle. No one stopped me because no one saw me. Once outside the room in which I had performed the autopsy on Bertha Spielsdorf, which thankfully was no longer under guard, I stopped. Closing my eyes, I felt for the *frisson* I felt whenever I was in the presence of Adam or Alina. There were three, two were on some levels above me. Adam and Fritz. The third was two levels below. And so I descended further into the bowels of Castle Dracula, wondering not for the first time, why I was risking all for a killer.

I knew the answer, of course, it was because Alina was not a killer. A fool perhaps but are not all lovers foolish. She did not deserve to be abandoned until Dracula forgave her, assuming he did not simply forget her. Or it could be that his show of mercy was just that, a show for the benefit for Adam and me and he intended for her to slowly rot away, alive and conscious until she went mad.

Or was it one last challenge? His smile suggested as much, silently asking me "Are you bold enough? Are you clever enough? Are you brave enough?"

This was my answer.

One level down, the stairs slippery with something the nature of which I did not care to think about. The feeling between Alina and me was now stronger. Another level, now no longer below, but to my left, down a hallway which Dante himself could not have imagined.

There were scattered torches, weakly lit, the light of each barely enough to reach the next. It was easy to remain in the shadows.

But the darkness was not solely mine. Things skittered in front and behind and though I prayed they were only rats, I recalled King Vlad's words to me.

"There are places here not even we dare to tread, where dwell horrors that will not be impressed by that pendant we hung around your neck."

Just as I thought this, there was a hiss behind me and something wrapped around my waist. It did not have the feel of an arm, but rather it was like living rope. A tentacle I realized, even as another grabbed my ankle and sought to trip me up and drag me into the darkness.

But thanks to the king's warning I was prepared. I dropped my bag. There was steel at my hip. There was silver strapped to my thigh. Only this time it was outside my clothes and not hidden beneath my clothes.

The tentacles tightened as I drew the silver and stabbed it into the meat of the ropey arm around me. The thing let out a cry of pain. When it released its hold, I turned on it, slashing what I could reach. A tentacle went for my neck. When I grabbed it and cut it away there was another cry of pain. Yet still it persisted and made the mistake of again grabbing my waist and pulling me to it.

But this time I was facing it. With both knives now drawn, one of silver and the other treated with the elixir of life, I stabbed it repeatedly until I heard it fall.

Retrieving my bag, I took my electric torch from it and shone it on the thing I had just defeated. I wish I could report that it was unfamiliar to me but I cannot. It was a creature that had been depicted in the painting Holmes had recovered in the Rossum case, a creature from a barren landscape where black suns cast dark shadows over things that could not have possibly existed.

Except that one did, possibly summoned by Van Helsing who could have used *The Book of the Way* to leave behind a trap for Dracula.

Of course, King Vlad had assigned guards to Alina's cell. Of course, the struggle had attracted their attention. Of course, one of them was Dimitri.

"Lady Watson, what are you doing down here?" he asked, although I was sure he knew.

"Killing that." I shone my electric torch over the…thing.

"My God," he exclaimed when he saw what I had killed. Dimitri's younger partner echoed him in Romani but in a different tone of voice when he realized that they had been alone with it.

"And may I ask, Legionary, what are you doing down here?"

"It is our duty to guard Alina," Dimitri said.

"I would suggest that it is now your duty for the two of you to tell His Majesty about that." Again I held my torch over the dead creature.

"Forgive me, My Lady, but I cannot leave you alone down here. I think you should come with us."

"I think not, Legionary." Even in the weak light from the torch, I saw Dimitri's partner reaching for his holster. "And remind your comrade that I have killed both a Bride and just now this creature of darkness. It would be no trouble at all to defeat the two of you. Now as a Knight of the Dragon I am ordering you two to inform His Majesty that his castle may be infested with monsters from *The Book of the Way*, monsters that neither ring nor belt can defeat. Go now. I will remain to carry out His Majesty's sentence."

After they left I located Alina's cell.

I had intended to pick the lock but in the darkness I had had no trouble in lifting the key from the younger guard's belt.

When I opened Alina's cell and shone my torch inside, she shrank back.

"Do not be afraid, Alina. It is I, Jane Watson. I have come to carry out the king's sentence."

On hearing this she was afraid until I explained. "The king

condemned you to be imprisoned until you were freed, I have freed you. Your sentence is over."

"But…"

"We have little time, Alina. Take this." I handed her the bag. "It contains clothing and money. Use one of the secret ways and go from here. Adam has a chalet outside of Geneva. He says you can use that."

"But what of the king?"

"I suppose if he comes to Geneva he can use it as well. But you must go. It is either that or the stake."

That convinced her. When she was gone I relocked her cell, sliding the key under its door. Its disappearance would be yet another mystery of Castle Dracula.

I was gone by the time the guards returned and after a thorough wash, I was back in my bed and in the arms of Adam Frankenstein.

Adam was with me when my coach arrived the next morning. Our parting was brief.

"One day," he said.

"One day," I agreed.

We embraced then he left me. As if waiting for him to do so, Luca then came out.

Without asking, he hugged me tightly.

"I will miss you, Lady Watson."

"And I you, Luca."

He then gave me a book and a letter. The book was a first edition of Stoker's *Dracula*, signed both by its author and its subject. The inscription from the latter read, "With thanks, D."

The note read, "You have ruined the boy. Take him with you. We give you our word we have released him." This time his signature read "Vlad R."

When I showed the note to Luca he stared at it in disbelief until I said, "What are you waiting for? Get in."

Frederick Morrow had elected to remain behind in King Vlad's service as so Luca and I traveled alone to the Borgo Inn. As we left Castle Dracula, I noted that the bodies of Dalca and Bogdan had been removed and that all the stakes were empty. I shivered slightly at the thought of what might have been.

Our return journey to Cluj-Napoca was, happily, uneventful, save for a warm and celebratory greeting at the Borgo Inn. Before leaving the inn, I stopped at the Church of Saint Sabbas to retrieve the silver cross Father Paul had given me. In turn, I gave it to Luca. When I placed it around his neck I held my breath. When it did not harm him I relaxed, knowing that King Vlad had kept his word about releasing the young man.

On our arrival at the aerodrome, I sent a not entirely truthful coded telegram to Holmes explaining that my mission had been more than successful and why. I then sent another telling him of a change in my travel plans.

52

We reached the Swiss village of Meiringen and checked into the *Enlgischer Hof*. When the landlord Peter Steiler saw my name he asked,

"Any relation to Sherlock Holmes's Doctor Watson?"

"John Watson was my father. This is Luke Morstan, my nephew. We will need two rooms."

"Of course, Doctor Watson. You've come to see the Falls?"

"What else?"

He laughed politely and had someone show us our rooms.

Luca, now Luke, and I spent our first few days making plans for his future and seeing the sights, deliberately avoiding the Falls. On the third day, I judged that enough time has passed.

"You know what to do?" I asked Luke.

"I do, Aunt Jane."

"Can you do it?"

"I have done worse at the castle and have had worse done to me. You can rely on me."

"Let us go."

It was a misty day and there was no one out but Luke, me, and one other.

"Wait here," I told Luke when we got the pathway that led to the Reichenbach Falls. Through the mist from the Falls, I walked on, stopping at the edge of the chasm.

As I looked into the cascade, I drew something from my pocket, a gold ring set with a reddish ruby, on the inside was an inscription in an unknown language.

She was, of course, waiting for me. Stepping from a place of concealment, Professor Moriarty in the body of Katherine Barnaby said,

"Well met, Doctor."

"Professor, I should have expected that you would be privy to any telegrams I sent Holmes and that you would be able to decipher even the most difficult of codes."

"Indeed you should have, Doctor. Why is it that you have the Ring of Gyges when your report stated that you had left it in the care of Dracula?"

"Elementary, Professor. When I handed the ring to King Vlad I used simple sleight of hand to substitute a well-made forgery."

"Very clever. And what do you plan to do with it?"

I held up the ring. "A certain Oxford professor of my acquaintance once fancied this as 'an object of power.' He may have been right. While I doubt that it has anything to do with invisibility it could be capable of binding us to the darkness. Or it may just be a ring. Either way, I plan on throwing it into the abyss."

From her pocket, Moriarty drew a pistol. "I think not, Doctor. Please, give the ring to me."

"You won't shoot. If you do, I will take the ring over the edge and it will be lost to you."

"A fair exchange."

"Tell me, Professor, it was you who arranged for an invisible man to free Fantômas, was it not?"

"Of course."

"And after Fantômas betrayed you, you ordered the invisible to follow him and to recover the ring and, if possible, to see to it that I did not return from Castle Dracula."

"Correct again, Doctor. Now which it is to be, you or the ring?"

Again I held up the ring. "Neither, I think."

A shot rang out, but not from Moriarty's gun. Instead, it came from a pistol which I had purchased in Cluj-Napoca and had given to Luke that morning. It was not the Webley but it sufficed.

My holding up the ring a second time was Luke's signal. He missed, of course. I had told him to aim away from us for fear that he might hit me. But his shot distracted Moriarty enough that I was able to close on her and wrench the pistol from her grasp. It was the first thing to go into the Falls.

Once again there was a struggle on the edge of the chasm, the Josephine of Crime against the Goddaughter of Sherlock Holmes. Despite her youthful appearance, she was the more experienced.

And due to the Elixir of Life which flowed through her veins, she was the stronger. It would have gone badly for me but for the silver bladed knife given to me by Father Paul of the Church of St. Sabbas.

I had drawn it just as we began to grapple and wasted no time in plunging it into her heart. She stumbled backward and once again Moriarty fell into the abyss.

53

Despite being guided by the *frisson* between me and Moriarty, it still took Luke and me two days to find my knife and her broken body. She was still alive, conscious, and in great pain. The look she gave when I pulled my knife from her body was either one of contempt or a plea for mercy. I did not care which. This time there would be no Moran to take her to a place of mercy. Nor would there be a mad doctor to reanimate her corpse. No, there was only me and my resolve to correct one of the worst mistakes Sherlock Homes had ever made.

Moriarty's pyre burned through the night and into the next morning. Once it was out, I scattered what remained. As for the ring, *it* was the replica. I threw it away.

54

"What's next, Aunt Jane?" Luke asked once we returned to the *Enlgischer Hof.*

"From here to Geneva, and from there to the Cluj-Napoca aerodrome, and then to home."

But it was not to be. A telegram from Mycroft was waiting for us in Geneva.

"Trouble in Casablanca. Go there at once. Contact the Prefect of Police for details."

So much for London. Once again, the game was afoot.

JOHN L. FRENCH is a retired crime scene supervisor with forty years experience. He has seen more than his share of murders, shootings, and serious assaults. As a break from the realities of his job, he started writing science fiction, pulp, horror, fantasy, and, of course, crime fiction.

John's first story "Past Sins" was published in Hardboiled Magazine and was cited as one of the best Hardboiled stories of 1993. More crime fiction followed, appearing in Alfred Hitchcock's Mystery Magazine, the Fading Shadows magazines, and in collections by Barnes and Noble. Association with writers like James Chambers and the late, great C.J. Henderson led him to try horror fiction and to a still growing fascination with zombies and other undead things. His first horror story "The Right Solution" appeared in Marietta Publishing's Lin Carter's Anton Zarnak. Other horror stories followed in anthologies such as The Dead Walk and Dark Furies, both published by Die Monster Die books. It was in Dark Furies that his character Bianca Jones made her literary debut in "21 Doors," a story based on an old Baltimore legend and a creepy game his daughter used to play with her friends.

John's first book was The Devil of Harbor City, a novel done in the old pulp style. Past Sins and Here There Be Monsters followed. John was also consulting editor for Chelsea House's Criminal Investigation series. His other books include The Assassins' Ball (written with Patrick Thomas), Souls on Fire, The Nightmare Strikes, Monsters Among Us, The Last Redhead, the Magic of Simon Tombs, and When the Moon Shines. John is the editor of To Hell in a Fast Car, Mermaids 13, C. J. Henderson's Challenge of the Unknown, Camelot 13 (with Patrick Thomas), and (with Greg Schauer) With Great Power …

You can find John on Facebook or you can email him at him at jfrenchfam@aol.com.

There has long been a debate among certain obscure and drunken literary scholars about whether **PATRICK THOMAS** was raised by Cthulhu, a leprechaun in a Manhattan bar, or two human parents. What there is no arguing about is that Patrick is the award-winning author of the beloved *Murphy's Lore* series, the darkly hilarious *Dear Cthulhu* advice empire, the *Bikini Jones* books, and the creator of the *Agents of the Abyss* series.

His over 60 books include F*airy with a Gun, By Darkness Cursed, Lore & Dysorder, By Invocation Only, Startenders, As the Gears Turn, Cryptid Fight Club,* and *Exile & Entrance*. He is the co-author of the long running *Mystic Investigators* series and the Jack Gardner mysteries.

Patrick is the co-editor of *Camelot 13* (with John French), *New Blood* (with Diane Raetz), and H*ear Them Roar* (with CJ Henderson). He wrote the first two books in T*he Wildsidhe Chroncles* YA series. As **Patrick T. Fibbs**, he has penned the Ughabooz picture and first reader books as well as the middle reader books the *Babe B. Bear Mysteries, the Undead Kid Diaries, Joy Reaper Checks Out* and the YA *Emotional Support Nightmare*.

Visit him online at www.patthomas.net and www.patricktfibbs.com.

The Past, Present, and Future of the Abyss!

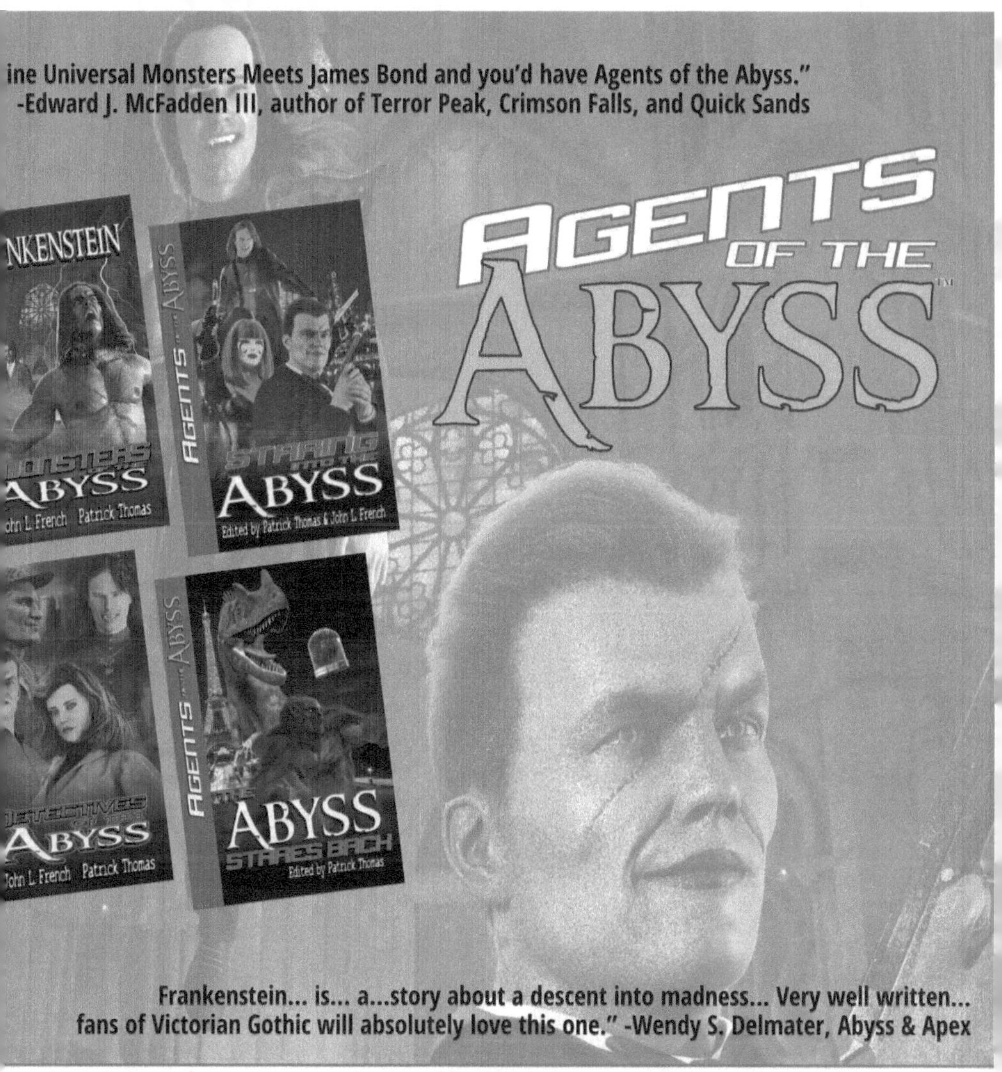

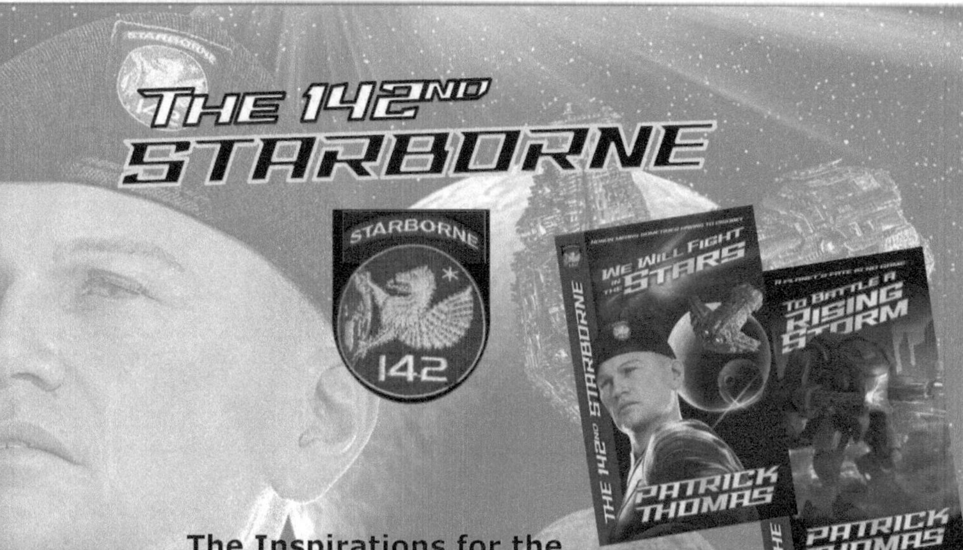

DOWN THESE
MEANS STREETS
of Magic & Monsters walk the

MYSTIC INVESTIGATOR

PAST SINS

Bad Cop...
No Donut

Monsters Among Us
a Bianca Jones collection

THE GREY MONK
SOULS ON FIRE
JOHN L. FRENCH

THE NIGHT MARE STRIKES
"THE NIGHTMARE IS COOL!"
-MICHAEL A. BLACK, AUTHOR
OF CHIMES AT MIDNIGHT
AND THE EXECUTIONER SERIES.
JOHN L. FRENCH

There Be Monsters
Jones collection
JOHN L. FRENCH

IT'S A CRIME
TO MISS THESE
GREAT STORIES!
from author
John L. French
WWW.PADWOLF.COM

ou can't
et better
than 13!

APOCALYPSE
13
DEFCON 1

MERMAIDS
13
TALES FROM THE SEA

Camelot
13
Edited by
John L. French and Patrick Thomas

LUCK
13
EDITED BY EDWARD J. MCFADDEN

THE
WILDSIDHE
CHRONICLES • VOL.1-6
OMNIBUS
No teachers. No parents.
School is out...of this world!
PATRICK THOMAS • JUDITH TRACY
TONY DIGEROLAMO • MYKE COLE

EVEN THE TEENAGE
QUEEN OF DARKNESS
NEEDS A FRIEND

Even the teenage Queen of Darkness needs
A NYX SHIVE BOO
EMOTIONAL
SUPPORT
NIGHTMA
PATRICK T. F

More GREAT Science Fiction!

THE STARSCAPE PROJECT

As his quest begins, an artificial intelligence life form enters the galaxy and launches a series of covert attacks against the Empire. The Teconeans assume that the Federation is responsible, and galactic peace is about to unravel. As Stryker chases his nemesis into Teconean space, he finds himself thrown into the middle of the battle. Knowing that Earth will be the aliens' next target, Stryker must decide whether to let them destroy the Empire, or to join forces with his Teconean enemies against the invaders. The key to the mysterious aliens lies buried on the moon of Kennedy Prime, and it's up to Stryker to solve the puzzle before war begins. The fate of the galaxy is at stake.

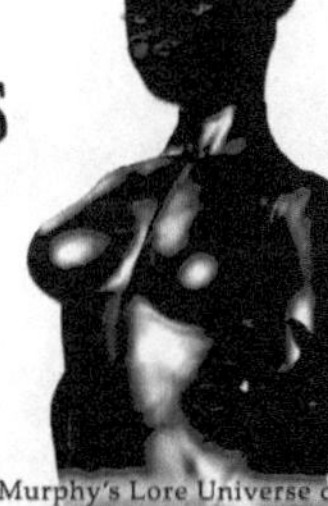

ZONE OF THE TENTH DGREE

In 1912, an alien ship crash lands in the Atlantic ocean, setting up a secret colony that remains undetected for centuries, allowing them to manipulate some of the most important events in human history -- from the sinking of the Titanic to the Bermuda triangle to global warming. Now, the technology of the 26th century has discovered the aliens' distress beacon, and it's a race against time as the Navy tries to stop a terrorist armed with a nuclear weapon from destroying the colony and triggering an all-out war as the mother-ship approaches

Now available from

PADWOLF PUBLISHING

Being *CURSED* to wear a bikini
Won't stop this Hero
From *SAVING* the world

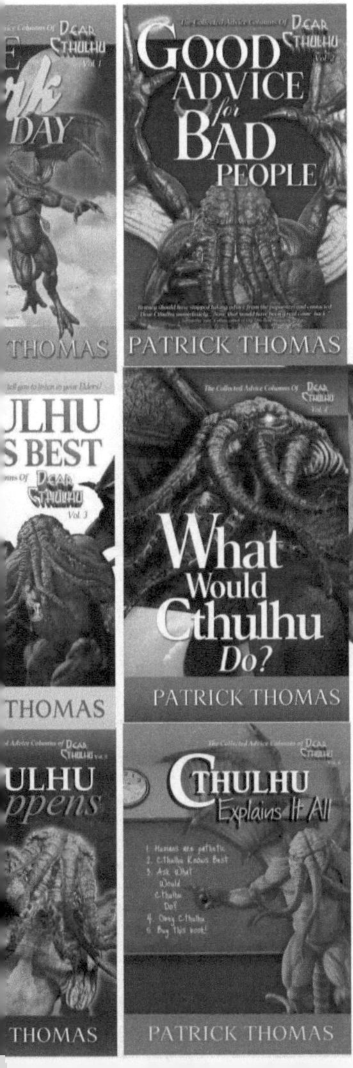

DEAR CTHULHU

THE ADVICE COLUMN TO *END* ALL ADVICE COLUMNS